Campbell Whyte

School Anthem

Li - ttle light shines bright - ly it gives a won-derous glow
light your way to stor - y land gent - ly lead you by the hand
step in to the sto - ry boat let your sails un - furl
sto - ry winds are blow - ing list - en one and all
list - en one and all
Old Mill Primary School

-FOR LIZ-
who makes
everything
possible.

Published by
Top Shelf Productions
PO Box 1282
Marietta, GA 30061-1282
USA

Editor-in-Chief: Chris Staros

Top Shelf Productions is an imprint of IDW Publishing, a division of Idea and Design Works, LLC.

Offices: 2765 Truxtun Road, San Diego, CA 92106.

Visit our online catalog at www.topshelfcomix.com.

ISBN 978-1-60309-412-2

Printed in China.

21 20 19 18 17 1 2 3 4 5

David Watanabe.
Next time you see me you'll need to look up to the night sky, 'cos I'm gonna be up in a space ship.
GOODBYE
Lilly Watanabe.
The next time you see me I'll be fixing one of your pets, maybe your dog.
I'm going to be a vet.
Ben Miller.
The next time you see me?
I'll be running my own patisserie with my big brother.
Amanda Holm.
Next time you see me? The next time you see me?
Maybe I could be, I dunno. I really don't know...
Nathan Dermott.
The next time you see me, I'm going to be making comics and probably writing them and drawing them and making video games as well and probably those pick-a-path books and, oh man, I just want to do so many things.
Laurence Baudin.
The next time you see me? I hope it will be in a book store.
Not behind the counter, like, writing books.

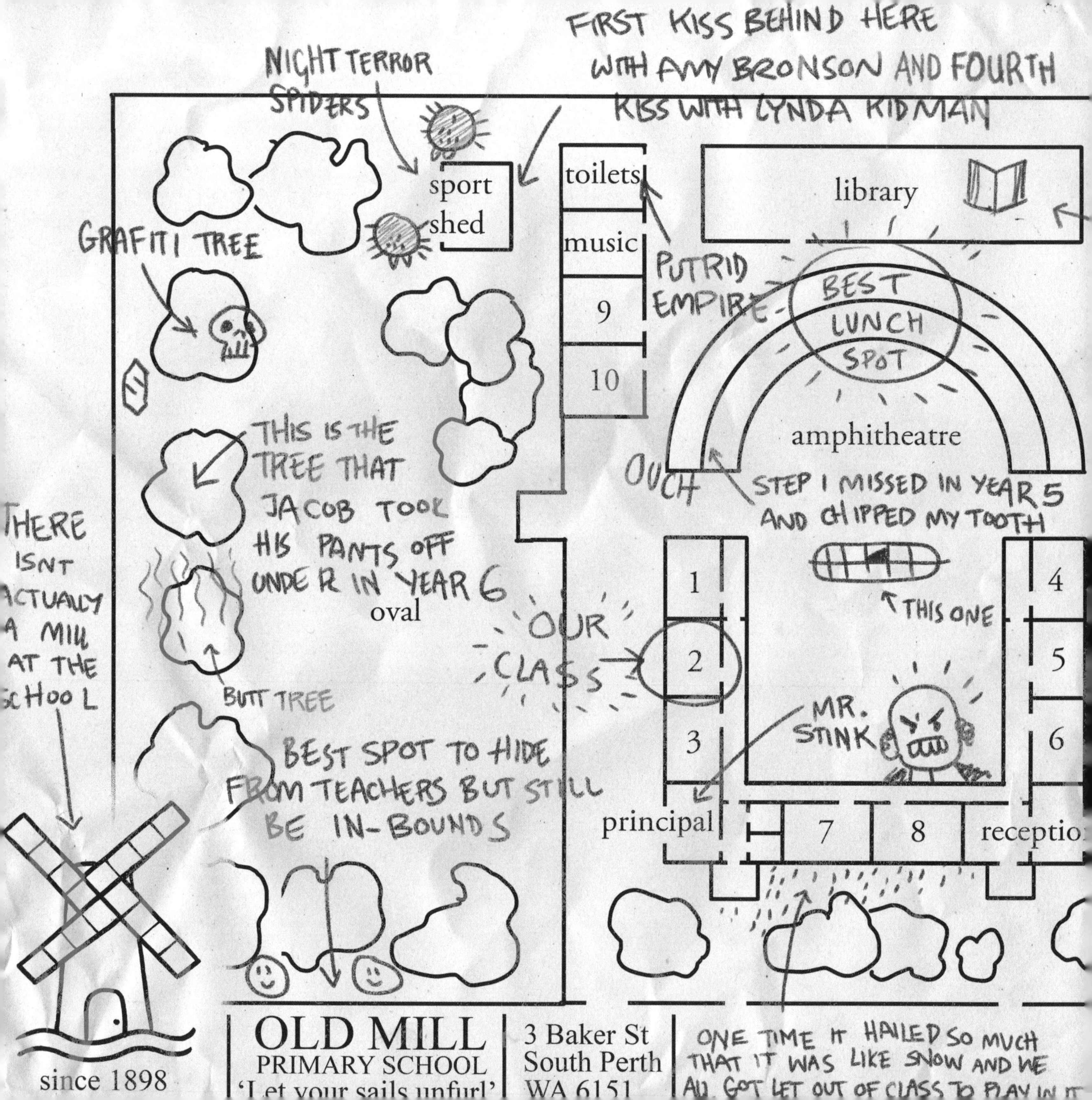
FIRST KISS BEHIND HERE WITH AMY BRONSON AND FOURTH KISS WITH LYNDA KIDMAN
NIGHT TERROR SPIDERS
sport shed
toilets
music
9
10
library
GRAFITI TREE
PUTRID EMPIRE
BEST LUNCH SPOT
amphitheatre
THIS IS THE TREE THAT JACOB TOOK HIS PANTS OFF UNDER IN YEAR 6
OUCH
STEP I MISSED IN YEAR 5 AND CHIPPED MY TOOTH
THERE ISNT ACTUALLY A MILL AT THE SCHOOL
oval
OUR CLASS
1
2
3
4
5
6
THIS ONE
BUTT TREE
MR. STINK
BEST SPOT TO HIDE FROM TEACHERS BUT STILL BE IN-BOUNDS
principal
7
8
receptio
since 1898
OLD MILL
PRIMARY SCHOOL
'Let your sails unfurl'
3 Baker St
South Perth
WA 6151
ONE TIME IT HAILED SO MUCH THAT IT WAS LIKE SNOW AND WE ALL GOT LET OUT OF CLASS TO PLAY IN IT

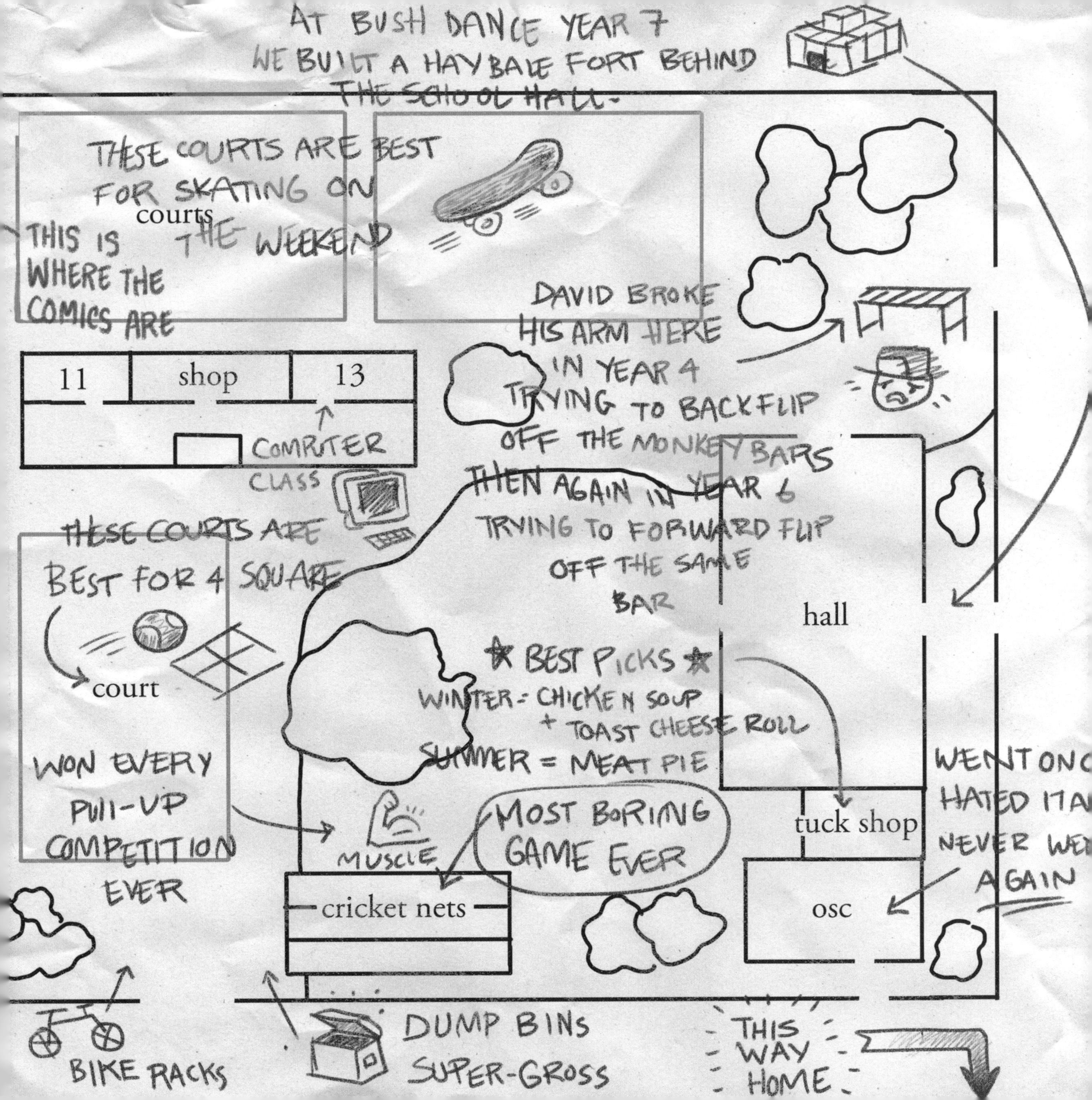

AT BUSH DANCE YEAR 7
WE BUILT A HAY BALE FORT BEHIND
THE SCHOOL HALL.
THESE COURTS ARE BEST
FOR SKATING ON
THE WEEKEND
courts
THIS IS
WHERE THE
COMICS ARE
11
shop
13
COMPUTER
CLASS
DAVID BROKE
HIS ARM HERE
IN YEAR 4
TRYING TO BACKFLIP
OFF THE MONKEY BARS
THEN AGAIN IN YEAR 6
TRYING TO FORWARD FLIP
OFF THE SAME
BAR
THESE COURTS ARE
BEST FOR 4 SQUARE
court
hall
★ BEST PICKS ★
WINTER = CHICKEN SOUP
+ TOAST CHEESE ROLL
SUMMER = MEAT PIE
WON EVERY
PULL-UP
COMPETITION
EVER
MUSCLE
MOST BORING
GAME EVER
cricket nets
tuck shop
osc
WENT ONC
HATED IT A
NEVER WE
AGAIN
BIKE RACKS
DUMP BINS
SUPER-GROSS
THIS
WAY
HOME

SEVEN!
SEVEN!
SIX!
SIX!
FIVE!
FIVE!
FIVE!
EeFfGgHhIi
GOODBYE
FOUR!
FOUR!
FOUR!
FOUR!
FOUR!

THREE!
THREE!
THREE!
THREE!
THREE!
THREE!
THREE!
THREE!
THREE!
TWO!
TWO!
TWO!
TWO!
TWO!
TWO!
ONE!
ONE!
ONE!
ONE!
ONE!
ONE!
ONE!
ONE!

RING
RING
RING
RING
RING
RING
RING
RING

15th December

You're not going to ring the bell?
That clanging piece of junk? No thanks.
But aren't you sad to be leaving?
No, I'm not upset. Not in the least, thanks, Amanda.
David thinks he's too good for primary school.
Well he's not going to high school. He's gotta repeat the year.
That's not true! Top of science, top of maths, top of geography.
Mum and Dad are worried about your social development.
They were going to tell you after Christmas.
Nice try. Nothing's going to put a dampener on me blowing this popsicle stand.
I can't believe this is it. We'll never hear the bell ringing again.
Popsicle stand?
The gentle clink of the chain in the wind.
That sweet tinkle.

The beautiful release from class.
Never, uh, never again...
Isn't that your house just over there?
Don't listen to the others.
I understand.
. Ugh. huh *sniff* ahg
awww...
It's what it represents, you bunch a banana slugs.
Wagh-ha-huh
those idiots
huh huh
Ugh, whatever.
Let's get out of here before the wailers start up again.
I'm going to m
you so much
oing to be ok
I promise.
I, uh, I don't, huh, want to, don't want to go...
We'll still see eac
other every da
I'm very much ready to leave this place.
WAGHH
Omigod Jenny
n't chuck a spack.
Jason is watching.
I don't even care.
WAGHHH-hurr...
Jason can take a photo.
-and i'll write every day and call every day, I promise, i promise -
Very much indeed.
AGH-HUR.
Oh yeah ?
What makes you think high school is going to be so much better?

I don't think, my friend,
I KNOW.
You don't think?
Har Har.
Listen to me, because I've got three words for you.
HOT-BABE-CITY
Look around you. There are no hot babes here.
At high school, it's all hot high schoolers.
They're "mature", if you know what I mean.
So they won't laugh at your jokes, then?
Not that sort of mature.
I mean mature in all the right places.

Oh right, I get you.
Well, Lilly sure is "mature", but in all the wrong places.

Eww, what?
Uh, you know. Umm...
What?
Don't talk about my sister like that!

HEY LILLY
DAVID, please don't please don't please don't please don't please don't please don't plasedon'tplase

Did you hear what Nathan just said about you?
-this is really important David, just shutup shutup shutupshutupshutupshutup

Weweretalkingaboutall thenewgirlsathighschoola howmuchmorematurethey'd becomparedtoallthegirlshere andhesaidthatyou'remature butinallthewrongplaces likeNOTintheboobs!
LALALALA

He said WHAT?

LAURENCE! Oh man, where have you been?
We were getting ready to leave without you.
I had to say goodbye to some people that aren't coming to the sleep-over.
You guys aren't my only friends.

That's Ben, he's been in our class every year since we were at Kindy.
I told you guys a bazillion times he was coming.
No.

Not him...

HIM!
PEPU!
Where have you been? What have you been up to?

Your dog? Hasn't he been missing for, like, months?
Heyo.
Hey man.

A couple of days, since Lilly left the gate open.
We'd better get him back home.

No, we just got him back! Can he come to the sleep-over?
He'll be good, I promise.

I don't see why not.

What could possibly go wrong with this scenario?
Right?

Right! We're all here, let's go already.
Laurence, Ben, you two can walk with us, you other two slugs can stay at least five metres behind us at all times...
...And don't try to talk to us or anything either.

WHAT? WHY NOT?

We only like to hang out with "mature" boys.

I'm totally mature! It's this banana slug that's not.

Five metres!

CHILDREN STOP CROSSING
WA POLICE TRAFFIC WARDEN
CHILDREN STOP CROSSING
You watch out.
It's going to rain, my boy.
WA POLIC TRA WA
You know the rain is coming, though, don't you?
Your friends don't. But you sure do.
What'd old man lollipop say?
I dunno ay.
LICE FIC DEN

I got a joke, you say, 'knock-knock'.
Knock-knock.
Who's there?
. . . very funny.

Ok, here's one, 'How many surrealists does it take to change a light bulb?'
Wa-what-a-lists? Your jokes are almost as bad as David's!

How can you say such a thing?
David's your brother.
Your TWIN brother.
UGH!
Don't remind me....

FIVE METRES!

SHHHHH, we gotta be quiet down here.
Remember that crazy old man who chased us with the broom?

You worry too much, Laurence.
Mr Slippers can go eat a rotten sock.

I'm never going to see him again anyway.

You excited about next year, Ben?

I guess so.
My brother said high school was pretty great...
It's gonna be nice having a familiar face there...

Someone I can count on...

Not like those two BANANA SLUGS!

20
km/h
BLACK
TEAPOT
CAFE

Court
R.S.L.
HALL
ROLLS
MADE
FRESH
TO
ORDER
Telstra
Telstra
67
ANGELO ST
Come in

Telstra
Telstra
Whoa, slow down.
Before we get to your place,
got a little surprise for you.
That's right.
We're going for one last
chip stop.
Thanks...

You idiot!
Laurence had already planned that himself.
Did you even read the invitation?
Yes!
Of course I read it.
I read it very well.
Of course you did.
fish monger
banana slug
PIZZA KEBABS
OPEN
PULL
BUS STOP

OPEN TIMES
GRAB A CHICO
SURF ON
MONSTBARIAN
LOVE
Hi, Jack.
FAMILY PACK
$20
"TOTAL" PARTY PACK
$30
GRAB A CHICO
"SURF ON"
HOT-HOT-HOT
50¢

Can we get...
uh, hold on...
Can we get five dollars worth of your finest chips.
WHAT?
Five dollars?
That's a lot of chips!
OPEN TIMES
Today's the last day for you kids, right?
Last day of primary school?
You guys are all excited today?
CHIPS
FAMILY
Summer holidays and then, it's Big Time!
That's the one.
mmm...
ugh, yea.
You kids are good kids. No trouble, not like kids from the other schools.
You're in here every day.
Look, let's make it special.
How about DOUBLE CHIPS for you?
$10 worth of chips?
Ew, that's a lot of chips.
YES! THANK YOU! We won't forget this!
That's really too kind, Jack.

Ahhhh.
Hey. I need you to do me a favour tonight.
What is it?
Nothing.
Is that a note?
No.
A letter of some kind?
No...
A piece of paper with words on it?
I guess you could describe it as such...
No, no way.
Why not?
No, you're not asking Lilly out tonight.
Who said anything about asking her out?
What's in the note, then?
Uh...
No.
Come on! She really likes you. If you give her the note she'll say yes for sure!

Puh-leeeease.

You've had all year to ask her out.
In fact, you've liked her through all of primary school.
So you've had all seven years to ask her out.
All of a sudden, you want to do it at the beginning of a double sleep-over?

Yes...
Yes. That's the general plan.

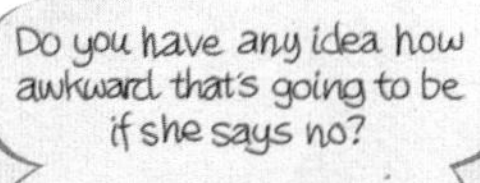
Do you have any idea how awkward that's going to be if she says no?

Or worse, worse even-

If she says yes. Then you'll spend three whole days not talking to one another.
Look, I don't want to go to high school without ever having a girlfriend.
I'll be the biggest joke ever.

Get David to give it to her.

I can't do that! He's her brother.

Oh look, just give me the note.
Yessssss.

Great, it's going in the bin.
NO!
Fine, it's obvious you're not going to help me. Some friend you are.
FAMILY

Soooo...
Yes?
I was wondering if you'd be able to give this note to David for me tonight?
Corazon/Ortolan
25¢ PUSH TO SELECT
25¢ PUSH TO SELECT
PLAYER 2
YOUR FRIEND IS BACK

You're not going to do anything stupid at my party, are you?
Oh what?
I said, you're not going to do anything stupid at my party, are you?
I dunno, probably.
What?
I might spill a drink or something.
A drink? What?
Yeah, look, I'm just saying.
And I was thinking of getting into a fight with Nathan...
WHAT? No fighting at my party.
I can't help it.
You can so help it.
He's just such a total dork-face.
Remember that time he hit me?
I wanna get back at him for that.
You mean that one time you were calling him a cheese wheel all week and he finally got sick of it and punched you in the head?
Yeah!
How can you be so smart and yet so stupid?

This one.
top 10
Ruby Rouge
Dynamite
Yeah, this one. Hahahahahaha, totally this one.
What are you guys doing?
AUTOTRADER
It's for our scrapbook.
You wouldn't understand. It's an inside joke.
Ugh, give me a break. He would so understand.
Anyone would understand.
They just cut out things they find funny and put them in a stupid scrapbook.
How dare you!
It's not stupid!
Ah.
Ten dollar chips!
Don't forget about me, hey kids?
You come back and see me.
Thanks, Jack!
HOT - HOT - HOT
FAMILY

Bye!
Wow, ten dollars worth of hot chips.
It's so heavy. Like a hot potato baby.
Look at it. All wrapped up nice and tight.
Let's see what's inside...
Arghh
Ah, so hot!

Hey. can we go in the pool when we get to your house?
Yeah.
Are we allowed to bomb off the roof in to the pool?
Yeah.
Are you sure? It's just, the last time I did it your mum freaked out at me.
Yeah.
I had to go home and everything.
Oi, cheese wheel. Show us these dorky books you got for your birthday.
What?
Those dorky books. I wanna see them.
They're not dorky.
Sure they're not...
They're fairy tales. It's all old fairy tales.
Yeah, these are definitely dorky.
Are they boring too?
No, David, they're not boring.
I did not ask for a dorky, boring book for my birthday.

They're beautiful
and scary
and strange
and surprising
and wonderful
and they make you think that everything here is terribly boring and suffocating.
That this place is going to grind you away into nothingness.

Is there fighting?
Some of them have fighting.
Are there robots?
You mongrel. They're set in the past. There won't be any robots in them.
One of them has a sort of robot bird in it, I guess.
HA!
I can't believe you're even asking about these books. You never read any fiction anyway.
Because it's stupid.
We're sending people up to Mars and giving people cyber hearts and you want to read about made-up fairies?
I don't get it.
I'm just showing an interest in my frien-
Gah! Stupid dog!
Do you think we'll still see each other much?
What are you talking about? We'll still see each other heaps. We still need you to come to Dungeons and Dragons.
I mean, we're going to different schools. My brother says he never sees anyone from his primary school any more.
What about Video Game Wednesdays?
Yeah...

Stop being so selfish, Laurence.
Amanda is going to a different school as well. You'll upset her with all your whining.
I'm just saying, things are gonna be different, is all.
That's all, everything's changing, and I'm going to be left behind.
You're going to be left behind? You're going to your fancy private school. You're going to shoot into the future and be a doctor or something.
In a few months you won't even remember us.
I don't want to be a doctor.
What movies are we getting out tonight?
Something scary. Something that will make you wet your pants.
I'll wet YOUR pants!
I hope it's not something scary.
Nothing scary, you slugs.
You guys don't even care about anything.
What do you mean we don't care about anything?
Dude, this party is going to be the best ever.
We're going to have the best time ever, and eat the most pizza ever.
And stay up non-stop for three whole days.
I'm not going to worry about some rubbish that's months away.
You're going to stay up for three days?
Is that possible?

Three whole days?
I don't know. But we're going to try.
It's raining?
It's summer, it's not supposed to be raining!
Is that thunder?
There'll probably be ball lightning tonight.
There's no such thing as ball lightning!
There is! Me and David saw it when we went camping!
PEPU!
Get back here!
Get back here right now!
Not in the river! Aghhhh!
Get back!
You hairy banana slug!
PEPU!
UUY!

Stop!
You'll get swept away too!
Noooooooo
Maybe we can reach him from the bridge.
He's just there!
Ugh, PEPU!
Can you get him?
Just a little bit closer...
Almost...

BACKPACKS

Because we were going for a sleep-over, our backpacks were filled with lots of extra clothes, toothbrushes and a few other things.

This is an incomplete list of our backpack contents. Some of it was lost in the river, but most of it survived. Strangely, there was very little water-damage to any of our stuff.

CLASS PHOTO

TOP ROW: 2nd David, 3rd Amanda, 4th Ben
MIDDLE ROW: 5th Nathan, 7th Laurence
FRONT ROW: 2nd Lilly

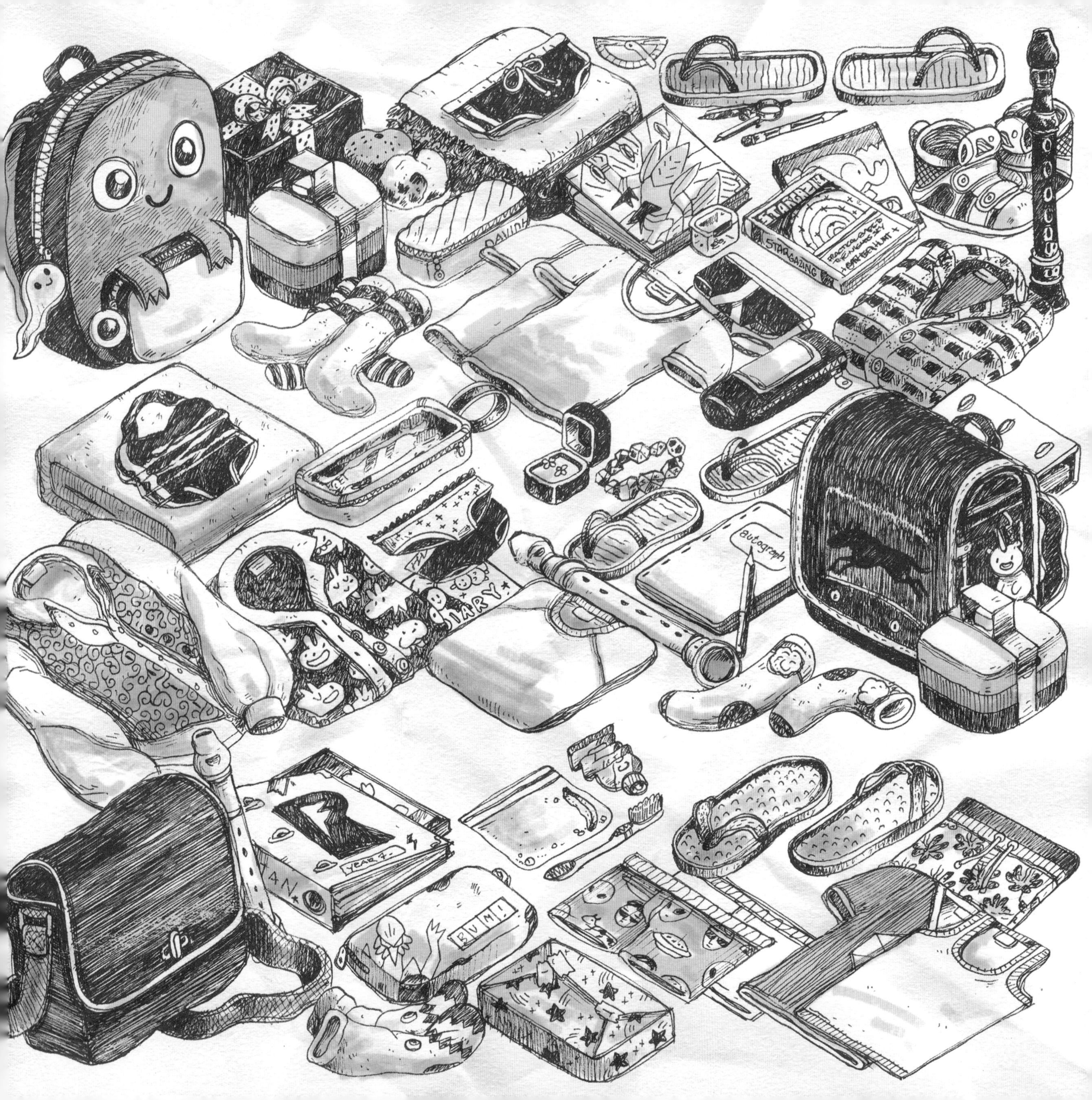
STARGAZING
Autograph
DIARY
YEAR 7-
BUM!

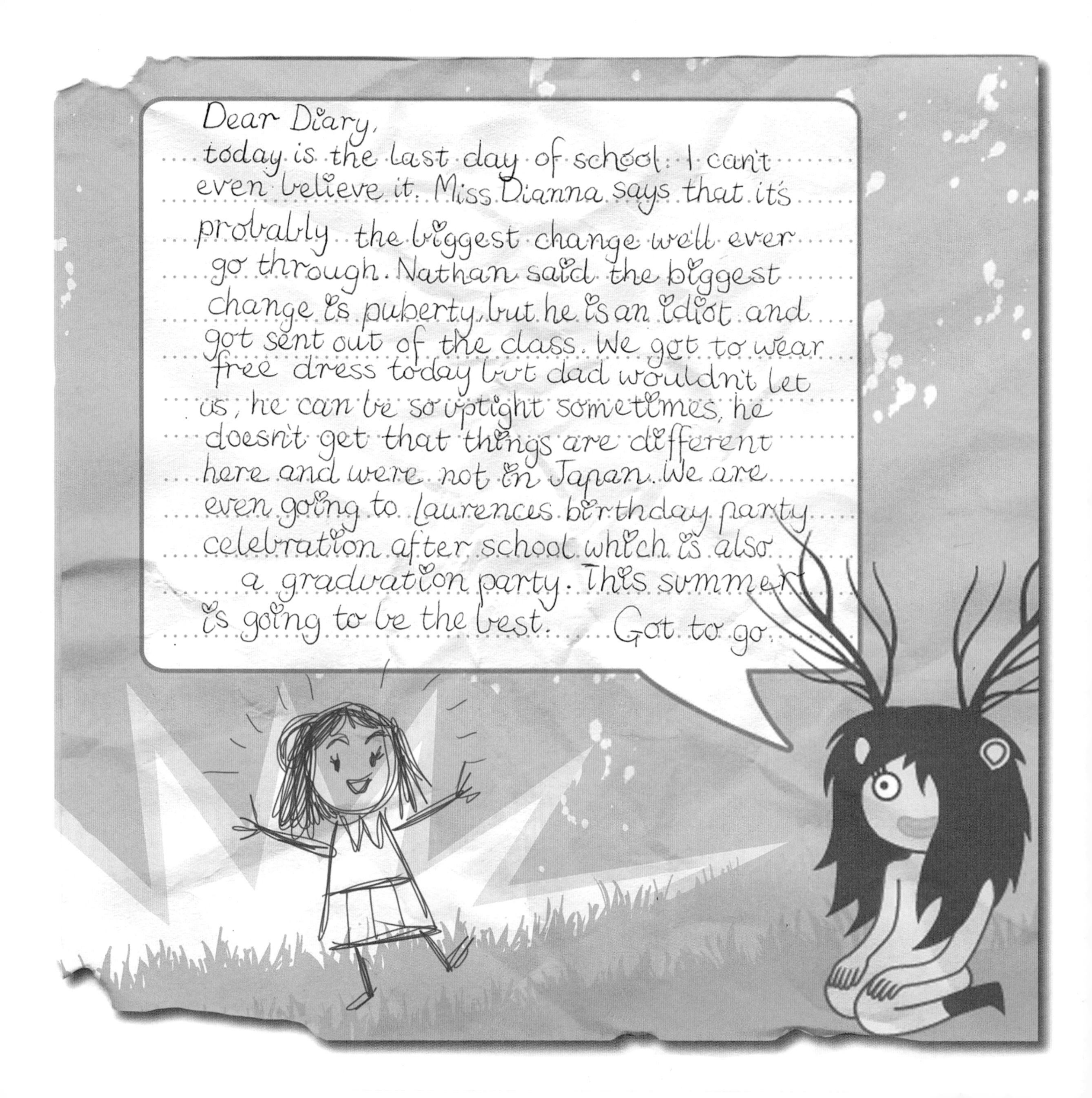
Dear Diary,
today is the last day of school. I can't even believe it. Miss Dianna says that it's probably the biggest change we'll ever go through. Nathan said the biggest change is puberty, but he is an idiot and got sent out of the class. We get to wear free dress today but dad wouldn't let us, he can be so uptight sometimes, he doesn't get that things are different here and we're not in Japan. We are even going to Laurences birthday party celebration after school which is also a graduation party. This summer is going to be the best. Got to go.

Double Luck Rainbow

RECIPE

1x double scoop ice cream cone
2x rainbow jelly snakes
2x scoops of vanilla ice cream

vanilla

GAHHH!

Gah, Pepu! SHOO!

Get outta here, you stinky thing.

WOOF
WOOF

Ar, quiet'n down would ya?
WOOF
WOOF

Where are we?

MUM!

MUM

Would you stop shouting PLEASE!
I don't need to wake up with you whining again.
Nuh-uh. You're just worried that you're going to be completely busted for not taking Pepu home straight away.
And letting him fall in the river.
And then making us all fall in the river.
And for shouting at me and EVERYTHING!
Where are we?

Lilly, what's going on?
I'm not sure.
I can't remember anything after we fell in the lake.
It wasn't a lake, it was some kind of sewer.

Are we at the hospital? Where is everyone? My stomach hurts. I probably drank some of that sewer water.
Calm down, Amanda, you're just nervous. Do you need your puffer?
Where's my mum and dad?
We're probably just at the hospital, it'll be ok.

Nah, this isn't the hospital. This is something else.
Remember the time I did that totally awesome back flip off the monkey bars and broke my arm? We went to the hospital then.
Gee, thanks for that, David.

Maybe we got washed up here by the river and this is some crazy hippie tree hospital.
Maybe.

That's the stupidest thing you've EVER said, EVER.
We're officially ignoring you now.
Fine, but it's not a hospital.

Well, what do you think, Ben?

Okie-dokie...

Where's Laurence? And Nathan?

I thought you were looking for "MUM" and "DAD"?
Hee hee.

Har har har.
But seriously, where are they?

Well, y'know. Thanks for all your help, guys.
I'm just gonna get some grown-ups and get us all home, ok?
Still not listening!

And you'll be totally busted, Lilly.
Totally.

You're AWAKE!
ARRR

You're going to love this. YOU'RE GOING TO LOVE THIS SO FRIKKIN MUCH!

C'mon, c'mon. Getup getup getup.
I've been waiting for ages for you slackers to wake up.

Let's go. This is the best thing that has ever happened to us.
Are we on telethon?
Where are we? Are our parents here?

Oh ho ho. No way am I telling you.
You have to see this with your own eyes.

C'mon, you trust me, right?
Sorta.
No.

Good enough. Everyone come over here and get on your garlands.

Oh, some of them fell off.
This one is for Ben.

David, here's yours.

Why do we have 'garlands'?
I dunno, it's wild, isn't it?
This is ridiculous.

Just relax and trust me on this.

Trust you? NO! You're always trying to make things 'awesome' and 'kick ass' and stuffing everything up.
Just tell me straight what is going on here.

David.

Knock it off, man. Just knock it off. That's it.

We'll just go along with it all, eh?
Hey?
You gotta calm it down.

Yeah, fine, whatever...

He's always acting like such a gooey banana slug.
I'm right here. I can still hear you.

OK FINE! Let's get on with it and find our parents. Because when we do you will ALL be busted anyway.
AND! We have a double sleep-over to get busy at.

Hrm, well, about that double sleep-over...

January
xxxi

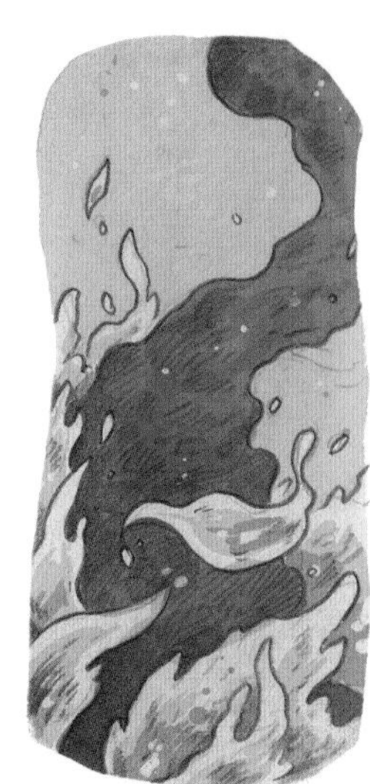

Yeah, check it out.
So I don't know if we're going to be making that sleep-over.

Welcome! Welcome!
A thousand welcomes, my dear Spirits!
TO THE FOREST OF THE PEACHES! That's us...
Come here! Don't be shy, we all just want to love you.

Wonderful, this is great.
Look at you two. I'm guessing the Spirits of Rising and Will?
Am I right?
I do so love to be right.

What's going on?
Just smile and play along.

Hahaha, Listen to this guy.
'Smile and play,' that's what I always say.
We're gonna get along just fine, we are. I can tell.

Nathan, thank you so much for bringing everyone out here tonight.
It's such an honour.
I see the spirits of Will and Rising...
...and here...

...these must be the spirits of the Beasts and Skies.

Oh, uh, yeah...

This is Lilly, the Beast Spirit. And Amanda, the Sky Spirit.
Beasts?

Lilly... Such a treat to meet you. To have you grace our forest with your divineness.

What a pleasure.

Now let's go.

Now, dear Spirit, Nathan has been filling me in on your long journey from the spirit realm to our humble little forest.
It sounds simply exhausting.
We have a lovely tree prepared for you all to rest in.

Now, do any of you know where the Spirit of Plenty has gone?
We asked Nathan, but he said he didn't know.

You mean Laurence? He's not with you?
No. How strange.

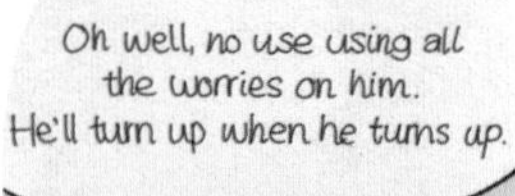
Oh well, no use using all the worries on him. He'll turn up when he turns up.

I once got lost visitng my bathroom.
I imagine crossing realms would require a great feat of navigation.

Oohhh, look at him go. He sure is fiery, this Spirit of Will.
Heh heh heh.

He's so sassy. The way he storms off like that...

Look at me! I'm so big and tough and strong!
Heh heh heh

hahaha.

Whoa.

Check it out.

They frikking love us.

I am pleased to introduce you to your branch elders.
Nathan has already met the Elder of Growth.

Yeah great. Everyone, get your things. We're outta here.
I see...

Yeah, you see.

Just like that?
No, exactly like that.

Hold on, these guys need us.
No.

Dude, what's going on with you?

I mean, I understand Amanda freaking out, Ben not saying anything, and Lilly playing it all so cool.
But you?

I thought you'd love this.

I'm going home, Nathan. We all are.

Sure thing, well...

Good luck with that...

Leaving? No, they're not leaving.

They're just tired. They've had such a long trip, you know how it is.

Imagine going to the crystal island and back. They must be exhausted.

Whoa, slow down there. You're so fast. It must be those big legs.

Now hold on, darling. It's getting dark out, and you haven't eaten yet, and you don't even want to know what's going on?

You Spirits can be leaving here whenever your selves want. But please, sleep on it.
Hear us out in the morning, then if you still want to go, then get on up.
Please don't do this in front of my people.

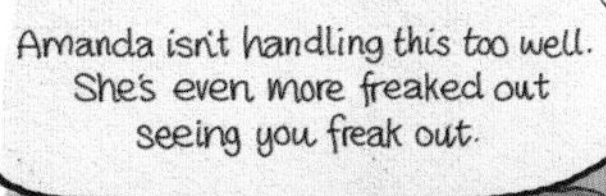

Seeing you walk out will kill them.

David.

Amanda isn't handling this too well. She's even more freaked out seeing you freak out.

Can you just pretend for the night? For her sake?

Big smiles.

Fantastic, eh? All that's ever needed are the right words at the right time.

This is a wonderful turn of events.
Just sparkling.

Don't worry, Elders. It was all simply the sleep talking. We'll do a big meet and greet tomorrow.

MY PEACHES RIPE! MY PEACHES SOFT!
WELCOME TO THIS MOST HISTORIC OF DAYS.

When the sun beats hardest, we ripen the quickest. Strong rains quench our thirsts. Every struggle is an opportunity.

Flowers must strain to unfold. Shoots must force their way up through the soil. Roots must dig and burrow.

We are gifted on this day with guests so rare as to have not been recorded since old tree times.

Their task ahead is not an easy one. But the forest knows best and would not send her own children to a foolish fate.

The tiny spirits are tired after their long journey and will be withdrawing to their tree soon.

But before they do, look at these faces, and see the faces of hope. Of optimism and great strength.

Know that with the spirits of the forest walking among us there is no force that can oppose us.

Peace will once again wash through the land and our home will blossom and rejoice.

GOODNIGHT!

Here we are.

'The Great Tree.' You can call this home for as long as you need.

Look at all the food here.
I'm starving.

Please, help yourselves. It's all for you.
As long as you stay, you will be provided for.

You aren't hungry?
Hrm?

You aren't hungry?
Do you have any hamburgers?
Erm, no, I don't think so. I will look into it... 'Ham burgers'.

Above are your bedrooms.
We thought it best if you chose your own.

HAHAHA! Top room!

Gah! Quick!
We can't let the boys get all the good rooms.

Well, we will leave you to get yourselves sorted.
See you bright and early in the morning.
We'll take you to your guild trees and help you get all set up.

Next door up is your room!
Check it out!

Arrrrgh, you gotta be kidding me.

I don't know how I can trust you.

But I'm going to have to believe you for now.

You had better not be lying to me.

What the hell is this crap here?
Huh?

Are you listening out there?
We're gone. Come morning we're gone.

I've had enough of this stupid magic forest crap and I'm taking everyone home to a double luck icecream!

Do you hear me, you devil?

That's a promise. From me, straight to your face.

Wait, what?

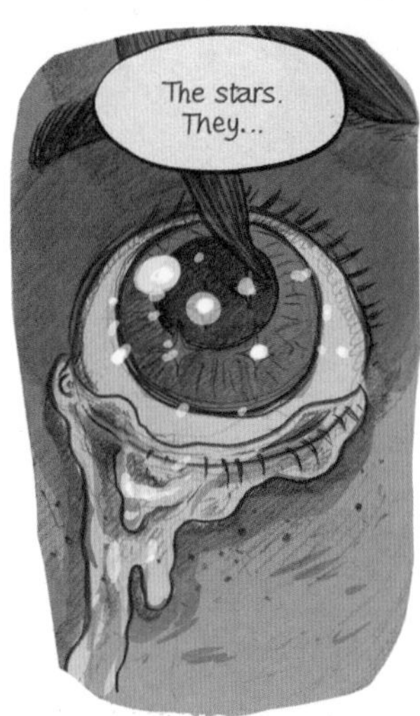
The stars. They...

Heh heh heh.
What's that? Who's there?

It's just me.

What are you doing out here? You spying on me?
I was out here long before you came along with your screamin' and pork choppin'.

Whateva you reckon, Ben. You're so full of it. Look, you better not tell anyone about what you heard or there's gonna be trouble.

You reckon?

Yea.

I reckon you better stop making all these promises you can't keep.

THE TREE HOUSE

Peaches within the village live inside treehouses, unique structures that provide them with all their basic needs. This treehouse has been grown especially for us, as we wouldn't fit a regular sized treehouse.

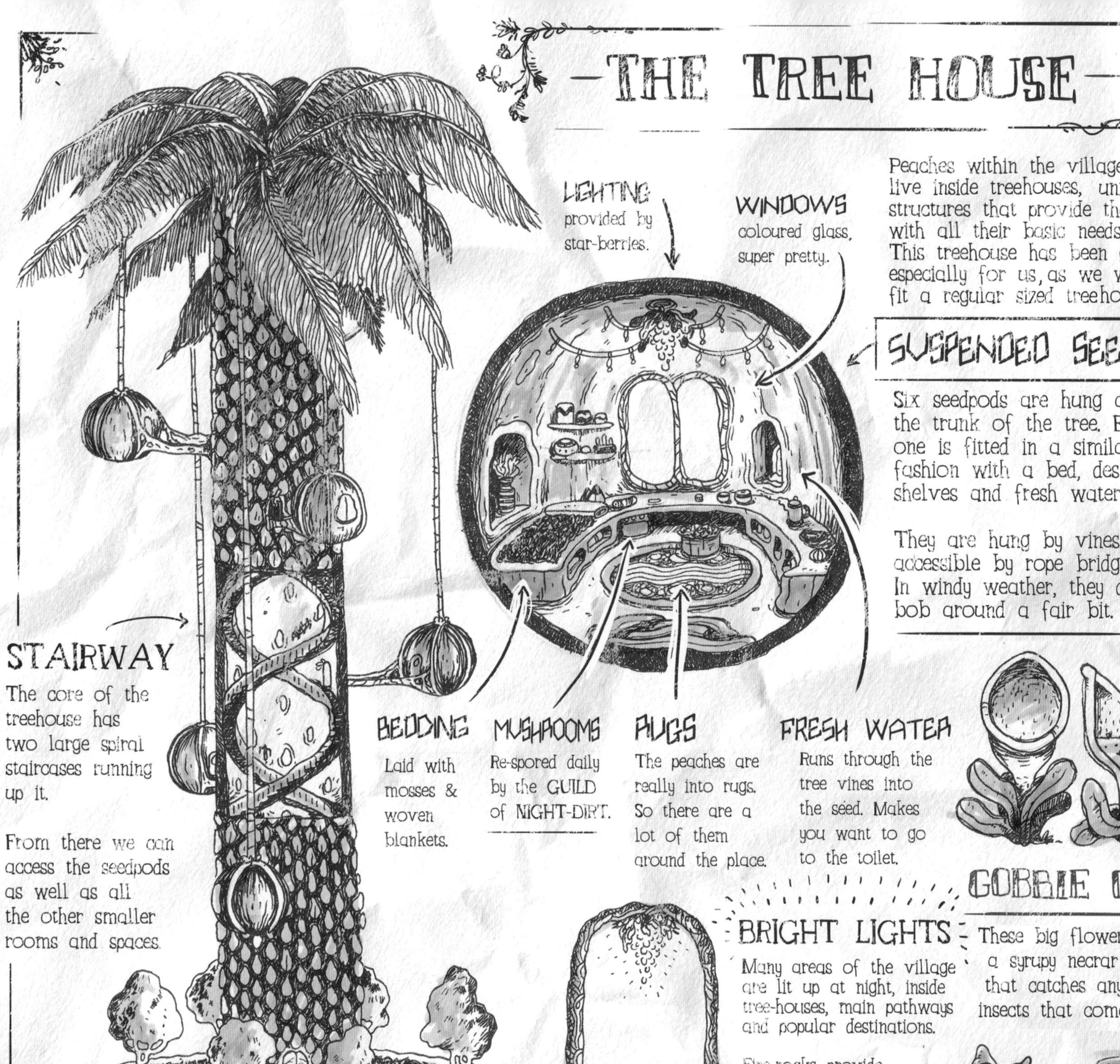

LIGHTING
provided by star-berries.
WINDOWS
coloured glass, super pretty.
BEDDING
Laid with mosses & woven blankets.
MUSHROOMS
Re-spored daily by the GUILD of NIGHT-DIRT.
RUGS
The peaches are really into rugs. So there are a lot of them around the place.
FRESH WATER
Runs through the tree vines into the seed. Makes you want to go to the toilet.
LITTLE DRIFTWOOD
STAR-BERRIES

SUSPENDED SEEDPOD

Six seedpods are hung around the trunk of the tree. Each one is fitted in a similar fashion with a bed, desk, shelves and fresh water.

They are hung by vines and accessible by rope bridge. In windy weather, they do bob around a fair bit.

STAIRWAY

The core of the treehouse has two large spiral staircases running up it.

From there we can access the seedpods as well as all the other smaller rooms and spaces.

GOBBIE CUPS

These big flowers have a syrupy necrar inside that catches any nasty insects that come close.

BRIGHT LIGHTS

Many areas of the village are lit up at night, inside tree-houses, main pathways and popular destinations.

Fire-rocks provide personal lighting, but more permanent light is provided by plants that have a natural glow.

~ LAND-CORAL ~

DIGESTION TREE

star-berries

At the centre of all Peach trees grows a DIGESTION TREE. This 'tree' is actually a complex growth made up of six different plants that all work together.

This is the HEART of the home. Peaches provide us with breakfast and dinner here which is varied. Throughout the day, Peaches keep snacking, so there's no formal lunch.

FAREWELL RING
The middle of the table has a pit where all food scraps are thrown where they are then eaten by the tree + table.

SOFT & HARD
Throughout the year the table will adjust its covering of vegetation.

REAR SEATS
Small stools with a mossy covering.

THE KITCHEN

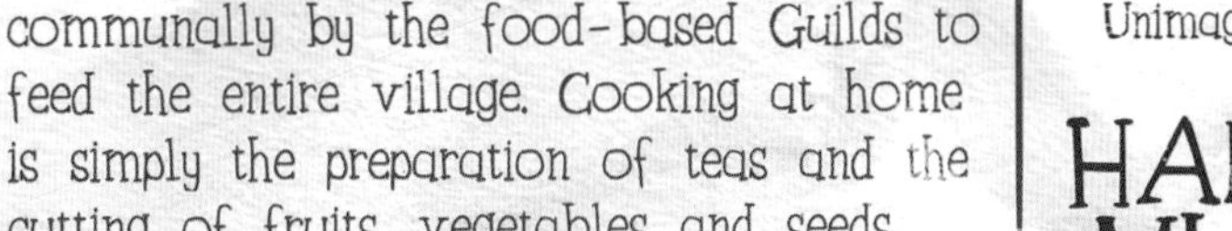

All tree-houses have a kitchen in them. These are relatively simple structures. The vast majority of cooking is done communally by the food-based Guilds to feed the entire village. Cooking at home is simply the preparation of teas and the cutting of fruits, vegetables and seeds.

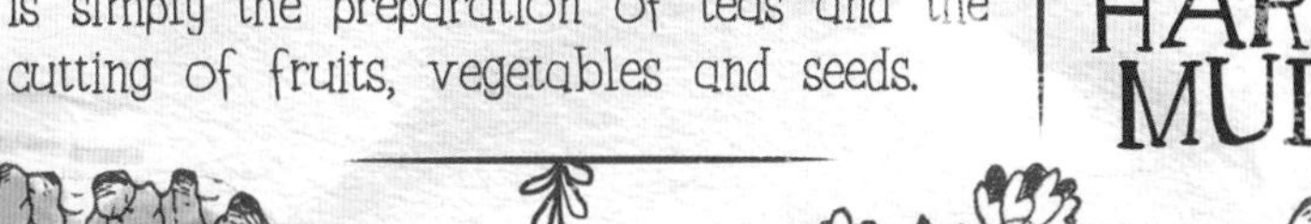

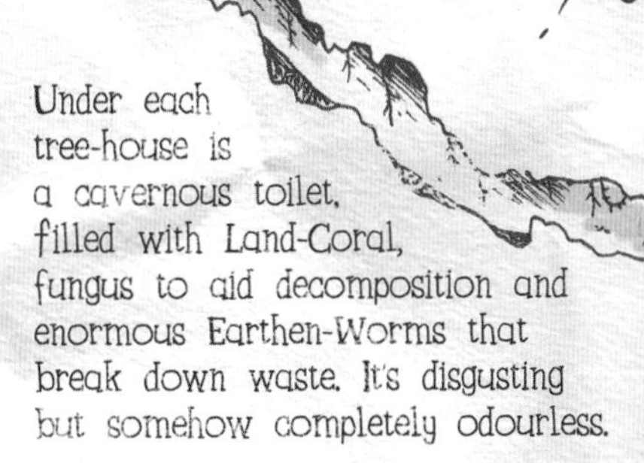

Under each tree-house is a cavernous toilet, filled with Land-Coral, fungus to aid decomposition and enormous Earthen-Worms that break down waste. It's disgusting but somehow completely odourless.

THE TOILET

COMMON FOOD STUFFS

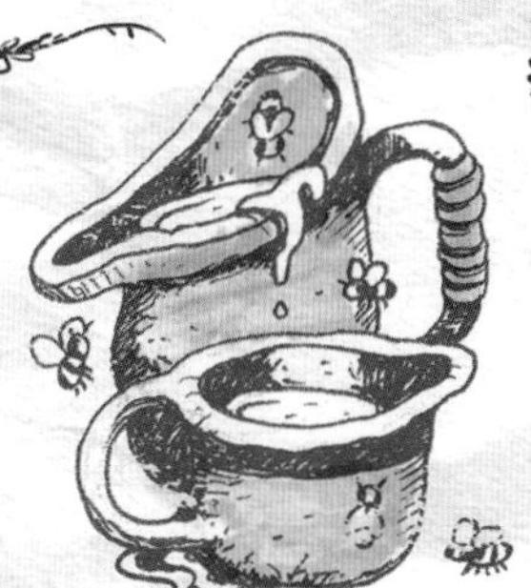

FRUIT JUICES

Almost all fruits are juiced to make a wide variety of sweet drinks.

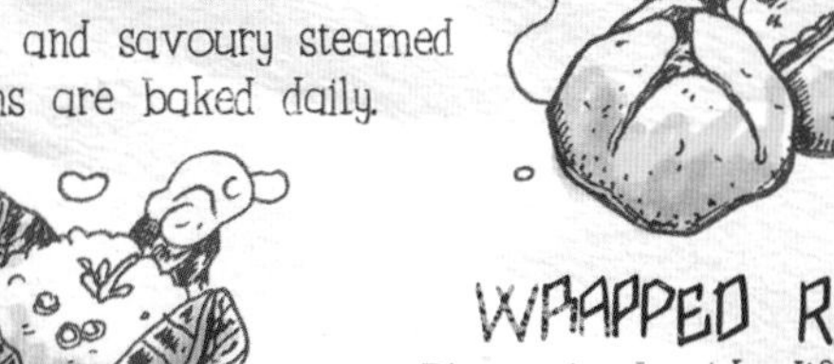

CLOUD BUNS

Sweet and savoury steamed buns are baked daily.

WRAPPED RICE

Rice, mixed with different fillings and wrapped in leaves.

FISH

The only meat that Peaches eat. Caught by the RIVER GUILD & Thunder Birds.

TEA

The major obsession of the Peaches. Drunk continually throughout the day.

FRUITS

Make up the majority of each and every meal. Unimaginable variety.

HARD MUD

Most foods are served on and in pottery. Vases, plates, bowls, cups in a huge variety of shapes are all crafted by the GUILD OF MUD.

Dear Diary

Miss Dianna said it was important to keep a diary even when we don't feel like it because one day we might want to look at it and see what it is we were thinking and we never know what's going to happen or be important.

I think something important has happened.

HERE - IS - THE - SEA
Here — is the sea — the wa — vy sea —
Here — is a boat — and here is me —
And — all the fi — shes swim — down be-low —
Wig — gle their tails — and a-way they go —

HRRmmm...

HUH?

EEEEEEE!

AH!
The what now? I don't, ah-
UGH!

Just, just like, stay down there while I...

Supreme ninja.

OHMYGODOHMYGODOHMYGOD OH MY GOD!

Oh, and of course...
The realest mystery...

Where's the bathroom?

FEBRUARY 1ST

Finally...
Literally the last room in this whole stupid treehouse.

Right?

EWWW!
No way...

So busting though.

GROSS gross
GROSS
Super double gross!

OH!
Flipping pancakes!

GIANT COMPOST WORMS?

I can't believe this...

Hey, have you been up long?
I didn't sleep.

You didn't sleep?
Have our parents come yet?
No one has come yet...

No one?
No one.

Well, what did the Peaches say? Didn't they say anything about how we were going to get home?
I dunno.

Well, what are we going to do?
I mean... what are we going to do?
I dunno.

What are we gonna do about getting home?
I mean, I didn't even see any Neighbourhood Watch stickers around or anything and -

I DON'T KNOW! I DON'T KNOW! I DON'T KNOW!

I'm gonna do everything I can to get us home!
But I don't know!

I don't know- I don't know- I don't know...

I know.

UGH!
GET OFF HER, YOU PIG!

I'm so sorry that my brother is a filth-mongering swine-trotter.
It's ok, we were-
I'm so sorry your face is a butt-butt

You have no idea how to treat a lady, do you?
HER?
A lady?
gross...

Just keep your festy sewer-mouth shut, David!
Look, we need to play along with whatever the Peaches say, ok?

Who knows how they'll react if they find out we're not really Spirits.
Ask no questions, and act like you already know everything.
So, just like we're at school...

Basically...
Fish-monger.

You wanted to stay up for two whole nights?
That would have been fun...
Morning, guys.
What's going on?

NOTHING!
David is just doing exactly what he's been told.
UGH...

GOOD MORNING!
Look at all this ENTHUSIASM!
This is what I had hoped for.
Goodness me, I think we'll see some real change coming from these beauties.

Great.
Cool.
Wonder.
Let's get this done.

He looks like he hasn't slept all night.
Maybes the Spirits are nocturnal?

Just play along....
It's just like theatre sports...

OH HAi!

WOW
Your hair looks even more like a cloud up-close.

Can I touch it?
Is it ok if I touch it?
Just a little?

WOWWWWWW
WOW
WOW!
WOW
Its amazing!

C'mon, let's go eat.
Everyone in the Sky Guild is growing to see you.

So, are there ghosts in this world?
GHOSTS?

Goodness no.
Those are only stories to scare the little buds.

What about Vampires?
Werewolves?
FRANKENSTEINS?!
Lilly said, `no questions`!

Sorry,
Never heard of any of those things before.
Maybe beyond the woven wall...
You Spirits would have a better knowing of these things, right?

Oh, of course...
BUT,
from our world, we can only, uh, see the realm we are responsible for...

Is that so? How interesting...
I always imagined we would be as fish under the water.
Shimmy shaking and darting.

Yessssss...
It's something like that...
WONDERFUL!
I do so like having my theories confirmed.

This is such fun.

The village... so, there's no electricity?
You must still be tired after your trip.
Let's get you a nice big pot of Morning Blossom tea.

That means, no internet.
No TV. No video games.

This is gonna suck eggs.

That sounds like fun!

WELL!
here we are.
This is our Emporium of Skyward Inquisition.
Where we try to learn what we can about your magical realm of the air.
Gimme a break...

Right-o! well,
see you all later tonight after orientation.

After the what-now?
We all gotta go to our guild trees.
I'm off to the hatchery.
Seeya.

We're gonna get introduced to the Peaches who care for our realms.
Who told you that?

My elder. Didn't yours?
Apparently there's some big drama with a mob of Bearded Dragons.

DRAGONS?
Don't worry.
I remember seeing a display of them at the Museum once.
They're really cute little critters.

Hee-Hee
Really, really.
The Peaches, look at them, they'd probably get spooked by a frog.

We can help them.

Until we figure everything out though, remember:
Don't ask any questions.
Don't answer any questions.
I can do it.

ANYWAY,
I gotta go.
See you at the night fair!

Night fair?

Are you ready, Dear Spirit?

Uh, I guess...

WELCOME!
WELCOME!
WELCOME!
Dear Spirit of the Sky,
Welcome to our main experiment room.

We are putting lots of effort into figuring out why some clouds turn pink at sunset.
Wha?

We have a few Peaches calculating how many clouds there are in the world...

And what clouds would sound like if they could talk.
COFF

There are so many great questions we can finally ask you.

We have
SO MANY QUESTIONS!

HA HAHA
LOOK!
This cloud looks like a big bird.

I guess...
kind of...

BLARRGHHH!

I mean, how BLARGDERFUL!
It means 'GREAT.'

'BLARGDERFUL'
I LOVE it.

Come sit down and let's eat some 'blargderful' food.
Did I use it right?

I would like to introduce you to our Cumulus Council.
They help grow our projects.
This is going to be great.
We can check our theories with you.

Uh, actually...

Are clouds really soft?
Or do they just look that way?

UGH...

Are clouds and the water that falls from them best friends?
Or mortal enemies?

UMmmmm...

When lightning comes from a cloud, does it tickle the cloud?

·HRRG·

Why cloud?

. . .

What cloud am I thinking of right now?

THAT'S NOT FAIR!
Our Dear Spirit isn't a mind reader!
TRUE.

Unless you CAN read minds...
EEEEEEEE...
CAN YOU READ MINDS?
Are our minds clouds?

-EEEEEEEEEEEE!

Maybe it was the Mancy-Buns?

WHOA!
It's a Spirit.

Hello.

I can see you, little one.
We're not all as blind as that fool Melaleuca.

Whatever.

Do you think we all believe in that stupid idea of Spirits?

There is a WAR coming with the Lizard Empire.
Did that useless rotten Peach tell you?

They've cut off all communications and trade with us.
Hundreds of moons of collaborations.
Done.

They've blocked all our fishing routes.
All our crops.

And Melaleuca would put our future in the hands of a snivelling MILKBORN like you.

I've seen creatures in the river that can swallow boats whole.
Sailors and all.

Do you ever go out on the water?

Do you ever go swimming?

OH HAi!
How is everyone going-a-go?
I've been looking all over for you, Dear Spirit.

You catching up with good ol' River-Elder?
I bet that was a basket of laughs.

What a big softie you are, my friend.
SOooo SQUISHY.

OFF FISHING AGAIN?
HAVE FUN!

UGHHHHH-.

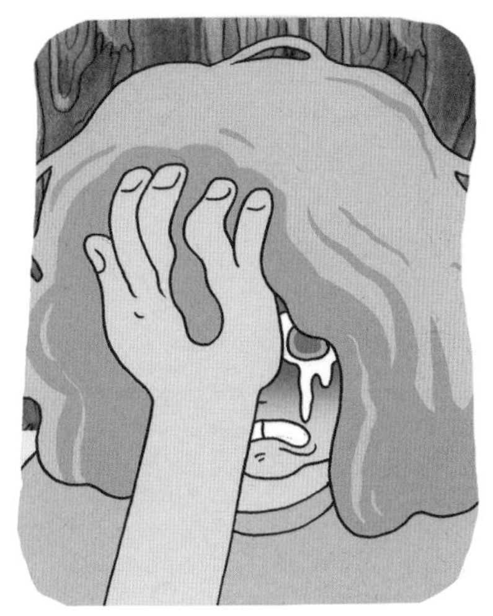

Have a tea.

It's good, yeah?
That's a **nimbus dream.**

Are you hungry?

I always feel better after a tea.

I... I don't know what I'm doing...

You...
You don't?

It's nice to know the clouds don't know either...

That it's ok just to be.

What a relief.

We don't need to know everything...

This is all River Peach territory.
They're in charge of fishing and taking care of the river ways.
Villea found you washed ashore on a morning walk.

They're a hard-working lot.
Not always the friendliest.

Prolly extra sore, seeings as the River Spirit didn't turn up.

We're meeting at FIRST TREE.
Just up ahead.

WHOA! it's Huge!
Yuppers.
Biggest tree we ever went an' grew.

Glad you could be making it.
Huh?
Hee hee!

Lilly!
Where have you been?
Everybud here?

Let's get started, then...

AWESOME!
COOL!
Hohohaw!

OHMIGOD!
Ben, what is THAT?
HUH?

Look at that HEDGE!
Topiary.

LOOK AT THAT!

Oh yeah, that's pretty awesome.
That's not 'awesome.'

I know exactly what that is.
Oh dear...

That's Archie
`BARGE ARSE'
Peterson!

The conflict between your realm and Archie's has been well documented in our tapestries.
But, every fruit on the tree is vital.
Tapestries!
'CONFLICT'?
He used to fart in my lunch box every day!

BEN...
LOOK...
IT'S ALL OF US...
ALL OF US...

EVEN 'STINK EYE' SUZIE!

Welcome again, Dear Spirits.
We had planned to do the sceptre ceremony last night, but, well...
things grew a little sideways.
When did they have time to do all this?

These things happen and always happen for a reason.
I heard that somewhere once.

The journey in front of you is going to be SUPER-SCARIFIC.
The Lizard Empire are a mighty strong lot.

Just last night they launched another sneaky-snook attack!
This time, pushing a large rock from the top of the cliffs onto our Thunder-Bird nesting site!
Last night?
WHOa...

A thousand sadnesses, as it crushed a nesting group in a terrific horror.
Did you know?
Pepu and I were the ones that found it.

In the first, I didn't want to admit that this... WAR... was growing.
But now it is starting to blossom, so that even my old eyes are seeing it.

River Elder has been whisper talking of being attacked up and down the water ways.
We have had to seal off the village in ways not done since the falling of First Tree.

We have even had to uninvite them from the Great Tea Festival!
Although it's unclear if they got our letters...

Thank you for answering our call.
We need your help to stop the attacks and bring us back together.

Great Tree has been storing your mighty sceptres, ready for your arrival.
And so, without further chitter chatter...

For our
SPIRIT OF GROWTH:

Your whispering sap.

AWESOME!

For the
SPIRIT of the BEASTS:

Your crook of night.

AND
a saddle for Pepu!

Thank you very much.
That's too kind of you.

To the
SPIRIT of the RISING:

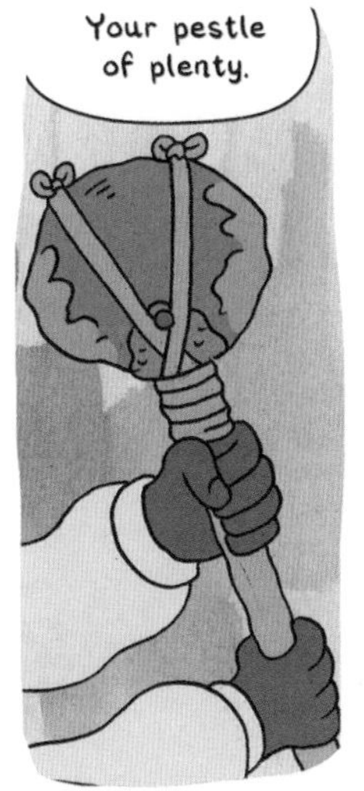
Your pestle of plenty.

It's heavy...

Thanks, guys.

To the
SPIRIT of WILL:

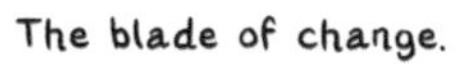
The blade of change.

OH HELL YES!

I got the BEST present!

And for the SPIRIT of the SKY:
-UGGHH-

We, we tried, we've tried our best, but...

It's ok.
Your sceptre has remained just out of our reach.

We have this humble gift as apology.

Ummmm...
Once you and the other Spirits collect your sceptre, you can then settle this terrific conflict.

It's a living map.

A what now?
A living map.

It's... alive...

Hi.

Sooooo...
this party has some pretty great food, hey?
HEY?

Where do ya think we are?

WHAT?
I don't know.
None of this makes any sense...

All the stars are back-to-front.
HUH?

Back-to-front.
All the stars, they're the same as at home.
Just back-to-front.
OH...

So... what are you doing tomorrow?

David?

Goodnight.

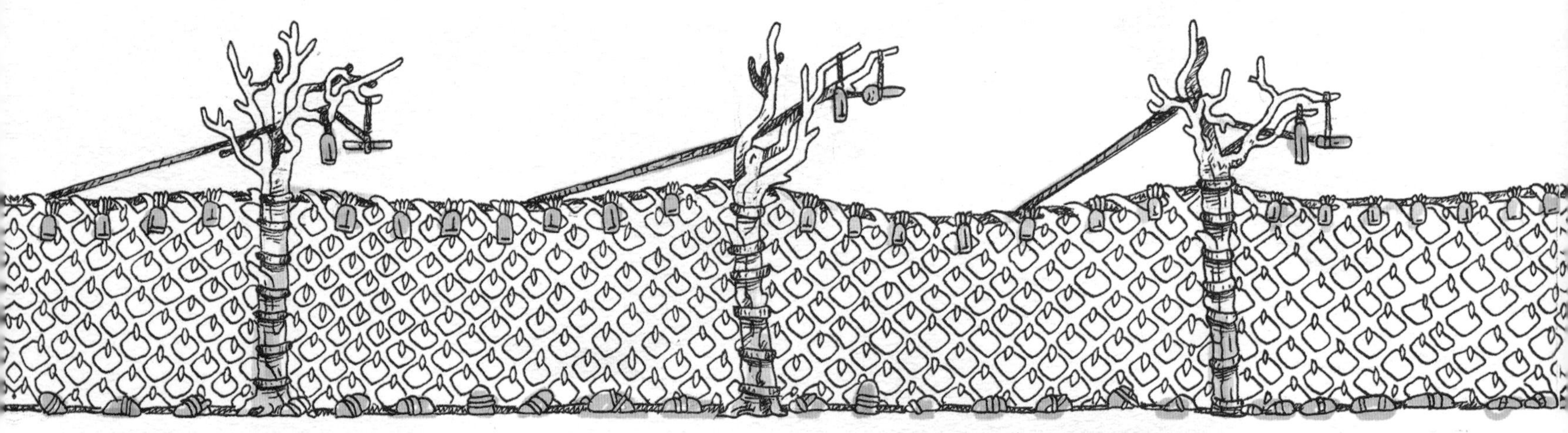

THE WOVEN WALL

Around the entire Peach Village is a giant wall of woven vines and dead trees. It has been designed to keep the village safe from predators such as herbivorous animals that threaten to eat important crops, structures and even the Peaches themselves. Since the conflict with the Lizard Empire has escalated, the wall has been reinforced.

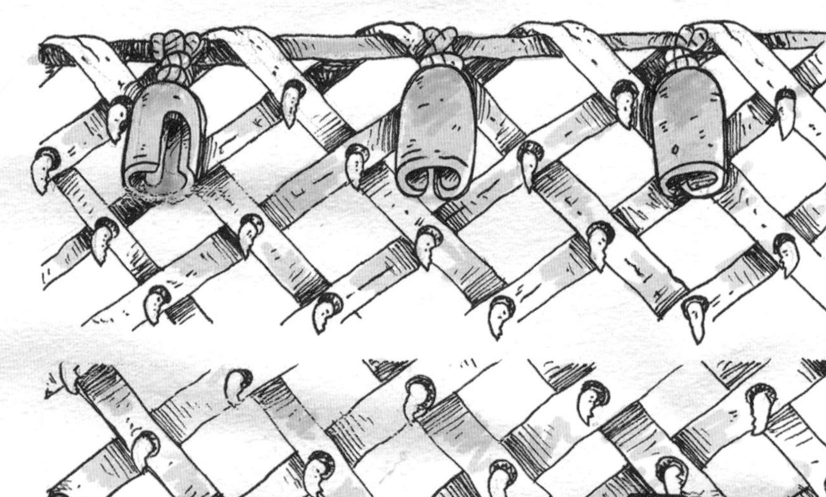

We have been told lots of times we are not allowed outside the woven wall. It's far too dangerous.

Small bells, stone weights & barbed hooks run the length of the wall.

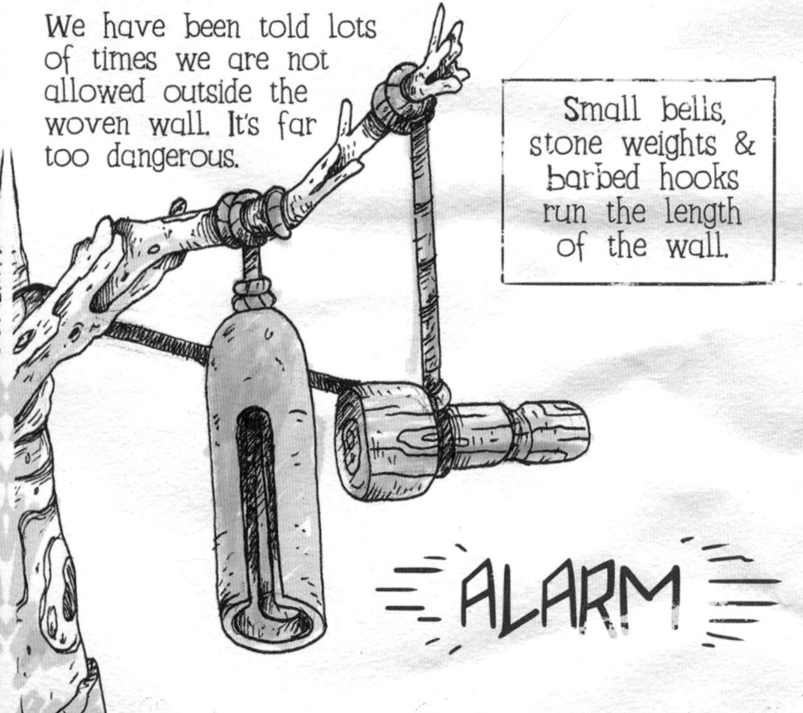

THE ART OF WEAVING

The wall is a complex structure that was sung into being by the greatest Peach Whisperers over many moons. While the tree posts are long dead, the vines are still alive, regrowing and recommitting to their task season after season.

Each length of weaving has a large chime connected to it that hangs from a post-tree. These chimes are loud enough to be heard throughout the whole village and will immediately alert everyone to an intrusion, although we haven't heard one yet. . .

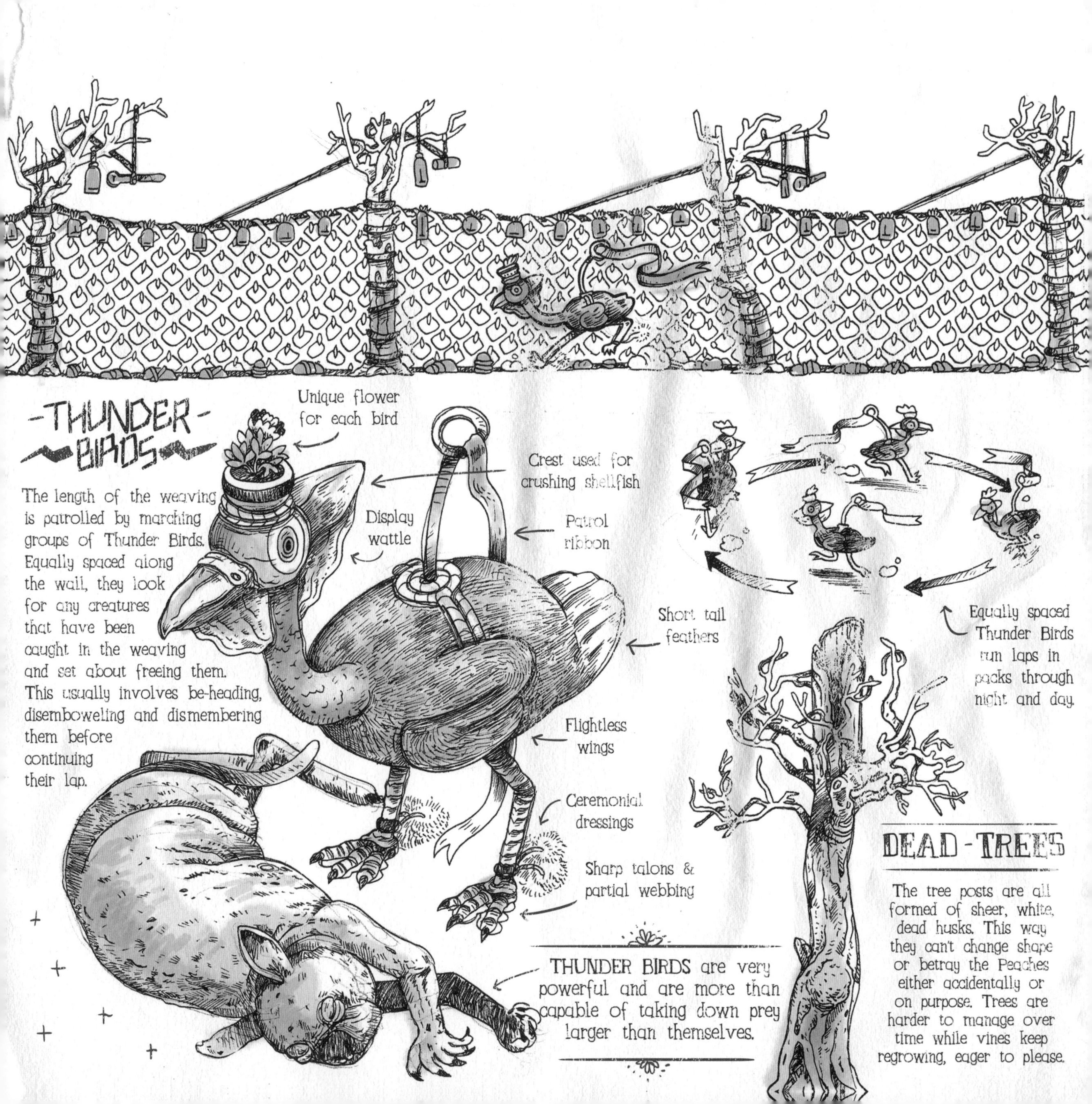
-THUNDER-
BIRDS
Unique flower for each bird
Crest used for crushing shellfish
Display wattle
Patrol ribbon
Short tail feathers
Flightless wings
Ceremonial dressings
Sharp talons & partial webbing
The length of the weaving is patrolled by marching groups of Thunder Birds. Equally spaced along the wall, they look for any creatures that have been caught in the weaving and set about freeing them. This usually involves be-heading, disemboweling and dismembering them before continuing their lap.
Equally spaced Thunder Birds run laps in packs through night and day.
THUNDER BIRDS are very powerful and are more than capable of taking down prey larger than themselves.
DEAD-TREES
The tree posts are all formed of sheer, white, dead husks. This way they can't change shape or betray the Peaches either accidentally or on purpose. Trees are harder to manage over time while vines keep regrowing, eager to please.

Dear Diary
We really are stuck here. I kept waiting for us to wake up and thought that when we went to sleep we might wake up but I woke up and we're still here.
The Peaches think we're magic spirits or something they even have a greatbig temple set up for us.
I'm supposed to be some animal spirit in charge of all the creatures. My guild elder Acacia took me to visit the giant bird nests. One of them was squashed! It was so sad. ☹ The Peaches all freaked out because the Lizards did it! That's why we're here, to sort out the Lizards then we get to go home.
egg
rock

water bombing
at serenity pools
found this
fluffy bum
me and my guild
elder Acuminatum
the laziest
dog of all
lilly + Amanda
were taught some
string games
freaky night jellies
a massive
flock of bats!

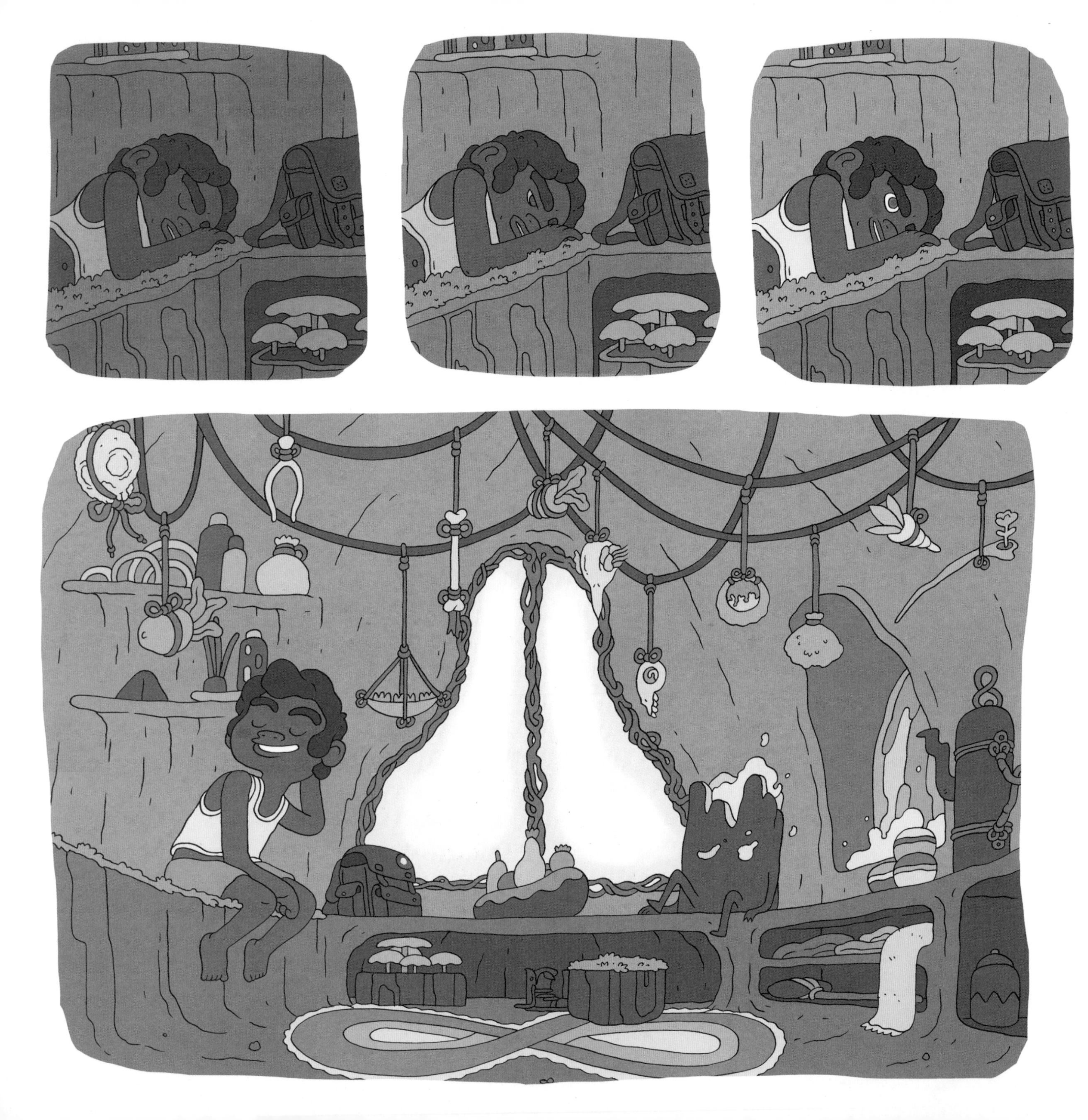

Morning, buddy.

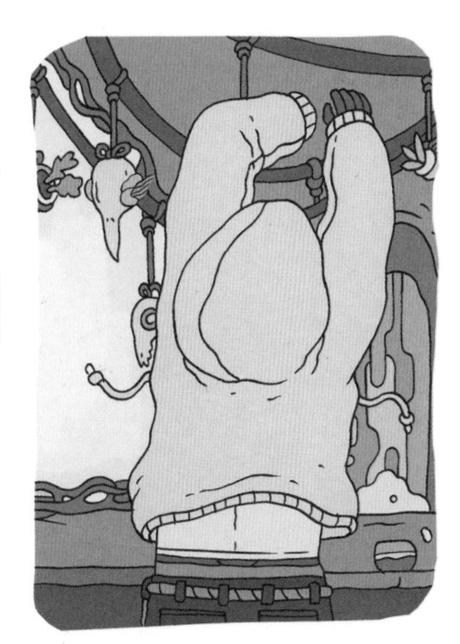

nom
nom

HuH?

No way.

The final ingredient!
Is beyond the weaving?

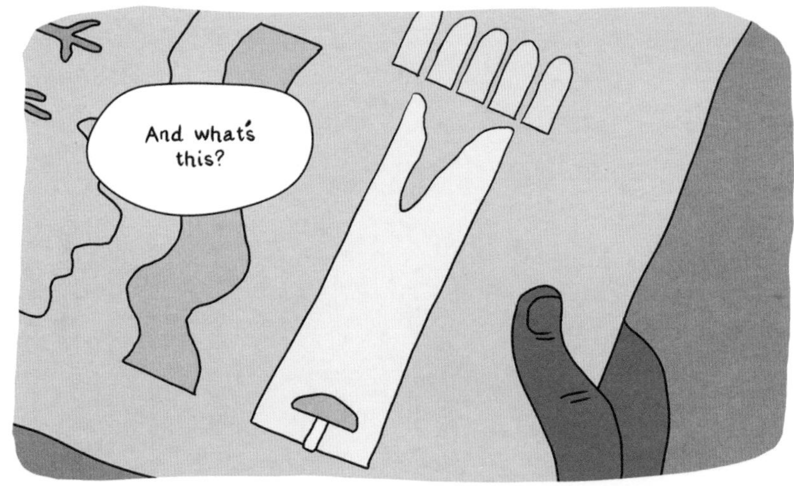
And what's this?

Hmmmmm...

One way to find out...

All I'm saying is

NATHAN,
I know how to brew my teas already.
I'm just making sure, ok?
The last few weeks you've been burning it.
I most certainly have NOT!

Well then, what do you call it?
`Steeping' it?
Thank you, AMANDA!

Morning.
Mornin'
I have NOT been steeping my teas.
OK OK, but let's be honest here.
They have been -

- pretty gross.

Like really really gross.

Remember the tea that made Amanda vomit?
yeah...

Gross.

There's nothing stopping you from brewing your own teas, Nathan.
Ha Ha Ha Ha Ha

I can make a pretty good pot of tea, if I do say so myself.

Elder Boronia said I've mastered four of the primes. Soon I'll start on the SECONDARIES!

I said, soon I'll start on the SECONDARIES!

THE SECONDARIES!

IT'S READY!
Who wants to try it?
WHOA!

m-m-ME!
I'll drink it!

No way am I wasting my tea on you, Nathan!
Amanda?
I'm kinda busy right now... soz...

Ben?

BEN!
QUICK!
Get your mug ready.

QUICK!
QUICK!
QUICK!
Uh, really?
EWWW...

AHHHHR...
That's a lot of tea...

Well?

Ok.
Here goes...

HUH?

Go on!
Don't be shy.
Is it supposed to change colour like that?

It's actually...
Not bad...
HA!

But MY tea is going to put all of yours to shame!
Oooooh...
WHAT?

OH YEAH, this festival belongs to me!

Say that again!
I double-dare you!
Ha Ha Ha Ha Ha.
You going?

HEY DORK FACES!
THIS STUPID "TEA PARTY" IS NOTHING!
David.

Every day you lot are either doing your DUMB chores, or-
WASTING your time brewing tea and giggling like a buncha babies!
I feel like I'm the only one actually trying to get us HOME!

I dunno, David, this Tea Festival is gonna be pretty awesome.
UGH!
No one cares, dingle-berry!
I'm trying to help...

This festival has NOTHING to do with us.
We get Amanda's sceptre.
We get these Lizards.
We get home.

How many times have we ever even seen these Lizards, huh?
Not once!

I don't even think they're real...
This whole thing is a joke!
After breakfast I'm gonna tell Melaleuca he's gotta send us back.

Where are you going?
To work on my tea!
I've got a festival to win.

OOOH,
Can I come with?
Sorry, Lil -

-gotta keep my brew a secret.

I just need this one last ingredient...

'spose I'd better warn Mal...
Don't think he's going to be happy about it though.
Maybe I should wait unti—
COME IN!

Come in.
Come in.
You can't sneak up on me like that, Ben. The plants tell me everything.
Now settle yourself in.
I have a mosting important question to ask of you.

I dont know if you're aware, but it's coming up on two months since you arrived on our shores!
Yeah, Amanda has been pretty vocal in keeping track...

Well, I feel like you know me well enough now to advise me on something...

A most delicate and importificate matter indeed...

This is of the greatest secrecy.
Uh, ok...

I trust that you are capable of being a discreet bee regarding what I am about to reveal to you...
Sure.

Alright...

Which do you prefer?

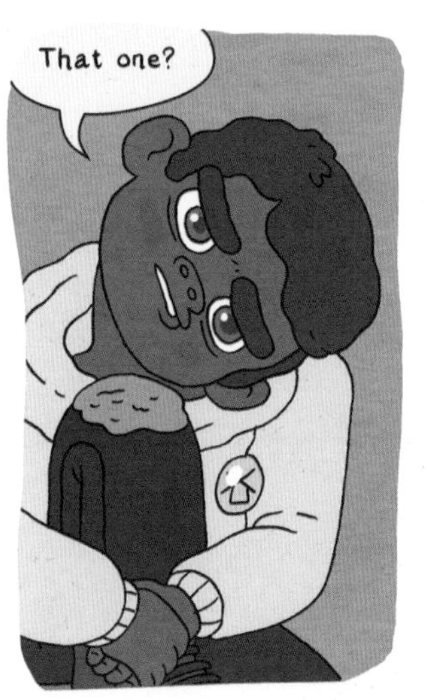
That one?

This one?

Yeah, that one...

Well that's a relief.
I've been worrying about this for weeks.

So I'm glad to be done with it...

Choice is a strange thing.

That's if you believe it exists at all.

Are you any closer to retrieving the Sky Spirit's sceptre?

NAH,
we've been to the island a few times, but it's so high up in that tree we can't...

It's driving David crazy.

He's coming down to see you today.
He wants to go home.

Well then, today will be like every other day.

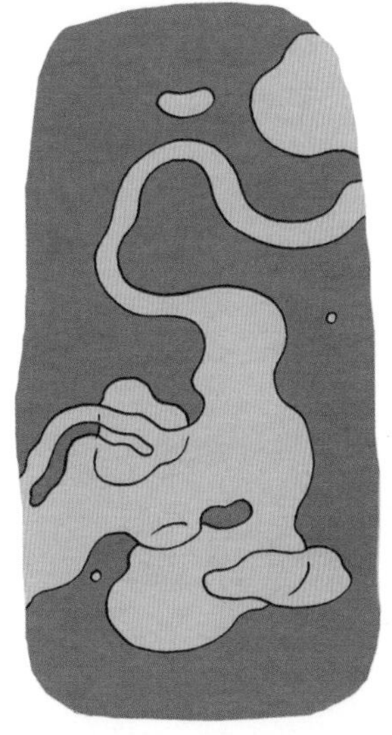

I suppose a certain amount of restlessnes is in his nature.

And how's your tea
for the Festival
coming along?

Welllll.
Now now, sweet blossom. There's need to be shy with me...
I know your secret!

WHICH secret?
UH, I mean, 'WHAT?'

Oh yes, your Elder told me EVERYTHING.
How hard you've been working on your tea!
And how you won't even share a taste!

OH! The tea...
I am much looking forward to the big reveal.

Some teas can ease an ache or calm a worried heart.
While others can send a Peach to sleep for a year, or make one live as if in a dream.

I wonder what you are brewing.
What change you will bring about in others.

Are we going home soon?

You don't really sound like you want to...

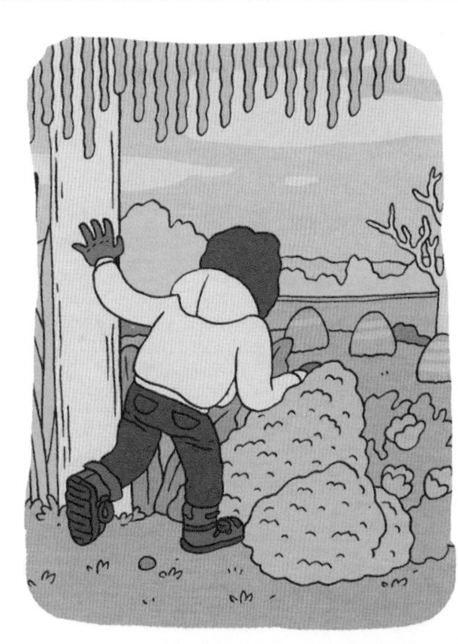

There we are...

One, two, three, four,
five, six, seven, eight,

nine, ten, eleven, twelve,
thirteen, fourteen,

fifteen.

A fifteen second gap...

GO!

UFFFFF..

MARCH
24TH

How many surrealists does it take?

Where have you gotten to?

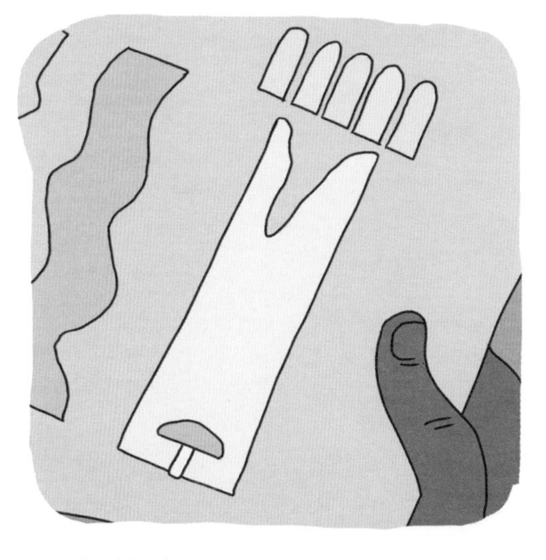

Carefully...

OOOOP...

BIG OOPS!

OOPS-OOPS-OOPS-OOPS!

AW GEEZ!

ARGGG

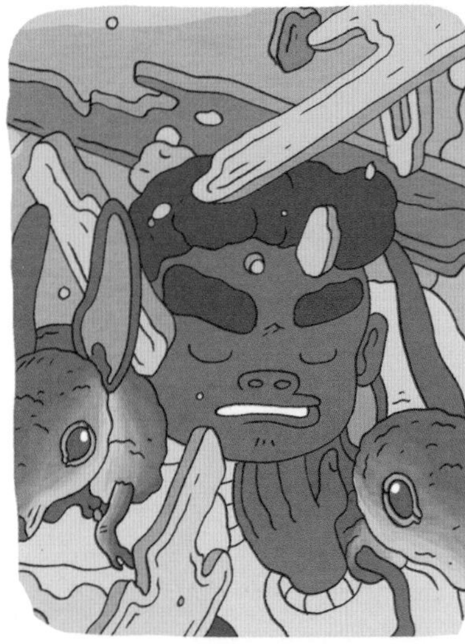

There you go, little fellas...
Wasn't so bad.

Just a little adventure.

Nothing like a bit of adventure!

-HUP-

OOFF!

Ha Ha Ha!

AH!
ERRR...

Uhhhh...

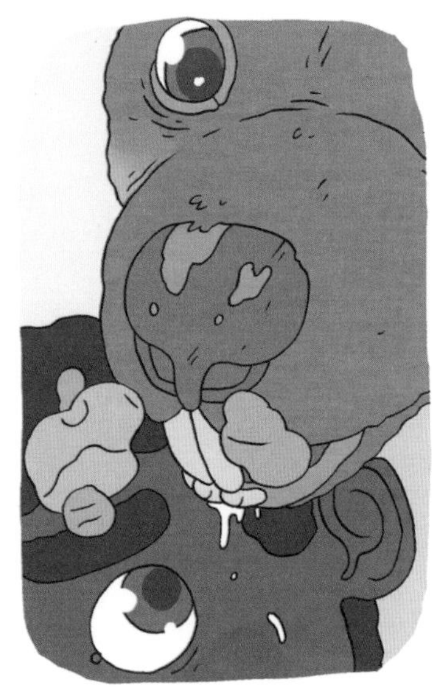

Heh.

Ha ha ha ha ha...

WHA-?

HiSSSSSSSSS

AAARRGHH!

HURRRRRRA
AWWWW

HURK

HARGHH

GLARGHAGLAR

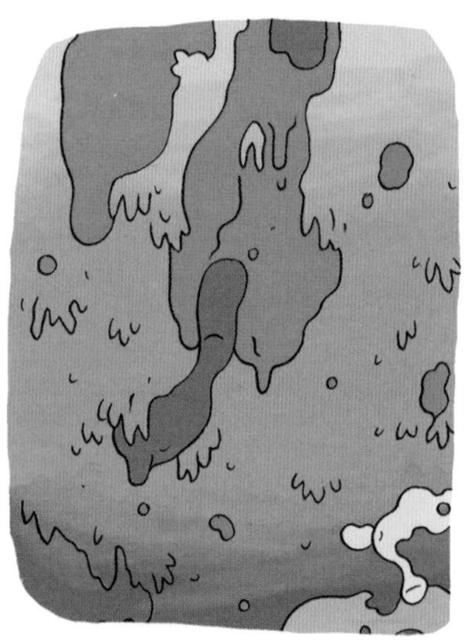

Huh
Huh
Huh

GAH!

SNIFF
SNIFF
SNIFF

GLARGHA!

HAGH
HAGH

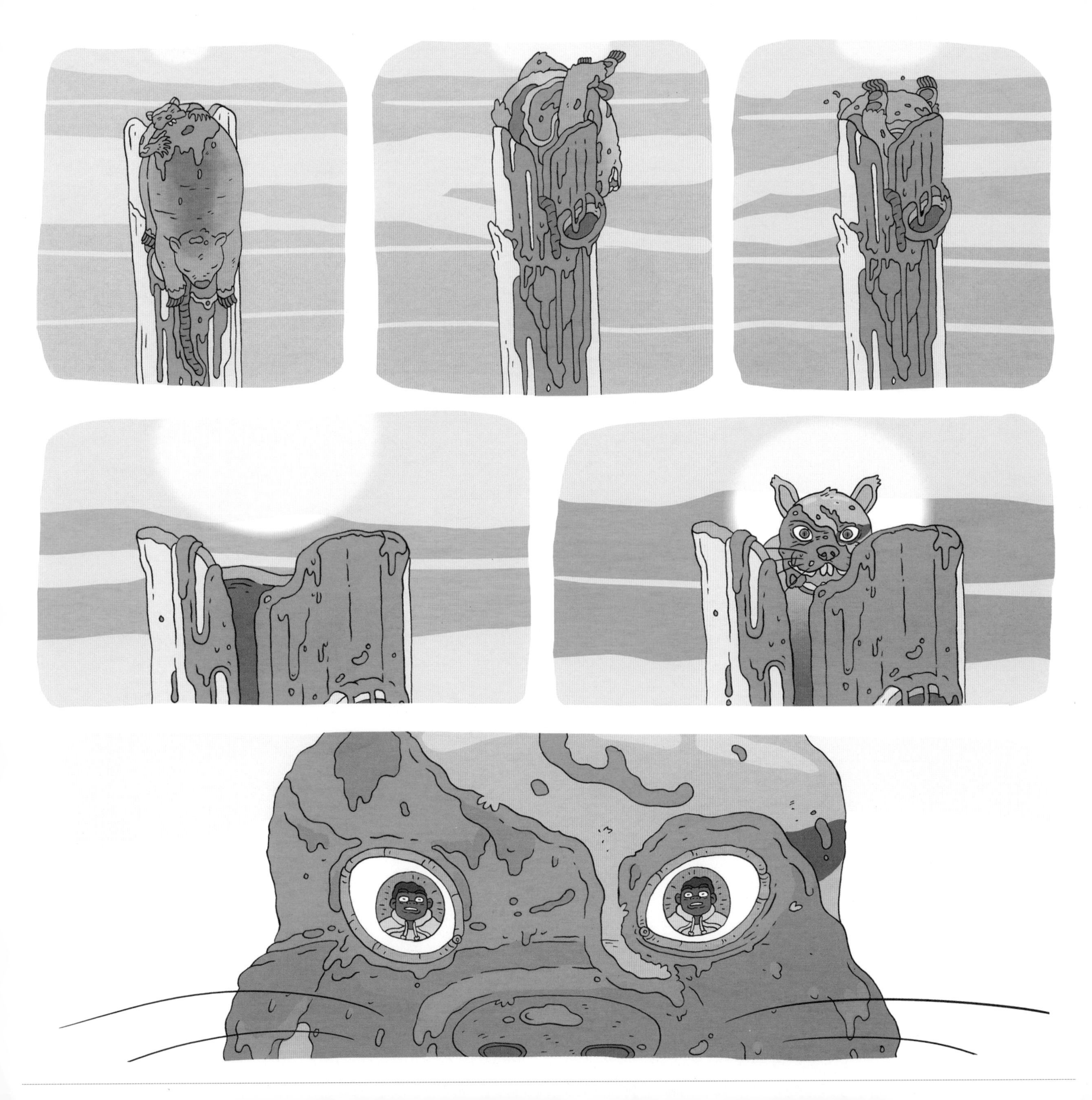

Heh...

Be seeing you.

You've been gone all day!
How did your 'SUPER-SECRET' tea go, then?
That's a super-secret, obviously...

Hey.
Hey.
How'd it go with Melaleuca?
UGH
Nothing! He's such a jerk.

There's dinner here if you're hungry...

BEN!
We missed you at the hot pools today.
Where you been?
OH, here and there.

WAIT!

You're not going to eat?
Nah, I'm not hungry.
Nobody knew where you went to today.
We had some sapphire drop lollies at lunch.
They were amaze.

WAH!
What happened to your jumper?
Oh, that-

All our clothes are getting so trashed.
Lilly keeps getting hers repaired by the Peaches.

And Nathan is wearing more and more Peach clothing.
Sooooo weird.
No way I'd ever wear that stuff.

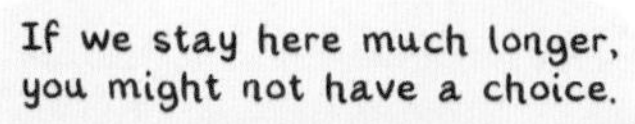
If we stay here much longer, you might not have a choice.

G'night.

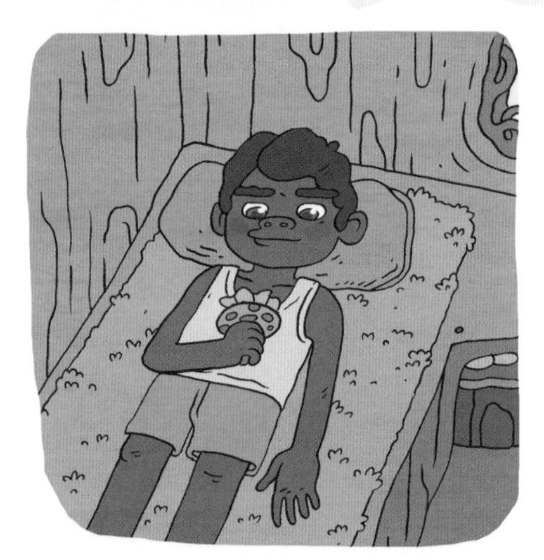

Gotcha.

night swimming
at the hot pools
Nathan and me got
totally lost in the
Amanda learning
some new songs
secret map
knowledge
my first
baked pink
rainbow birth
play.
we went out to
get Amandas sceptre
my hedge!

GROWING -A- VILLAGE

The entire Village of the Peaches has been created by the Whispering Guild without cutting, sawing, or building any structures. Instead, they ask the plants to grow into the shapes that are needed.

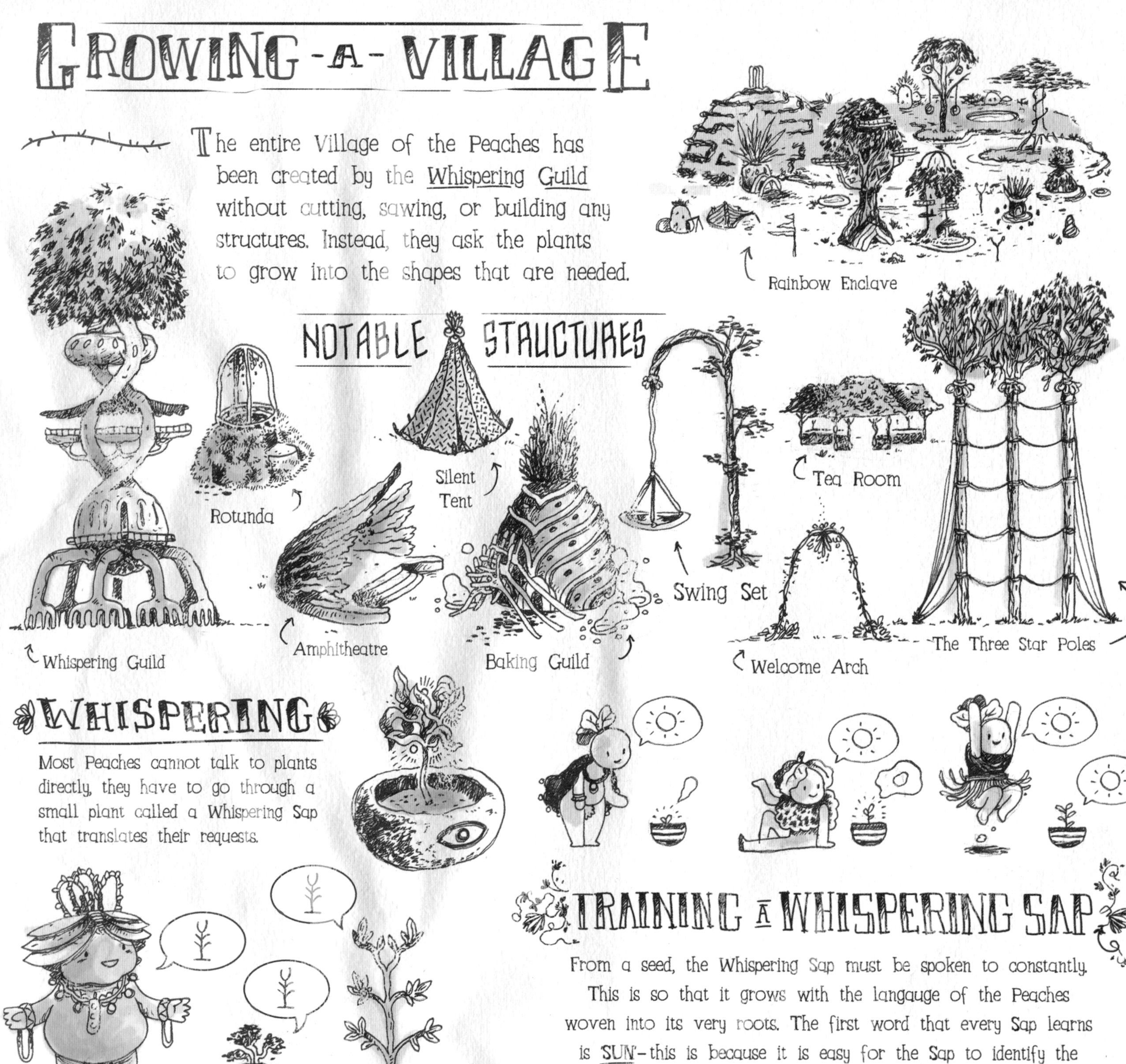

WHISPERING

Most Peaches cannot talk to plants directly, they have to go through a small plant called a Whispering Sap that translates their requests.

(example of a growth request being fulfilled)

TRAINING A WHISPERING SAP

From a seed, the Whispering Sap must be spoken to constantly. This is so that it grows with the langauge of the Peaches woven into its very roots. The first word that every Sap learns is 'SUN'- this is because it is easy for the Sap to identify the presence and absence of light and is of such great importance to the plant. Over time, it will begin to learn the shapes and sounds of other ideas and be able to translate them.

✳ NEGOTIATIONS ✳

There is always a degree of negotiation involved when asking a plant to grow into a certain form. Some plants are known for their general eagerness to help. These are often used by beginner Whisperers and for common purposes. Other plants are notorious for their reluctance to assist and sometimes even will grow in strange formations simply out of spite for the Peaches.

COLLABORATIONS

The vast majority of Peach structures are collaborations between multiple plants. This requires a number of delicate negotiations to take place. Sometimes the use of certain plants means that other plants cannot be used due to existing animosities. It is the Whisperers' responsibility to manage these conflicts to ensure harmony.

FIRST TREE

(before it fell to rot)

REBELLIONS TO ORDER

UNFORTUNATELY there are times when for one reason or another a plant grows in an undesirable manner. This might be due to malice, miscommunication or illness. Handling of these situations is delicate and best left to the DAWN COLLECTIVE of Whisperers.

(rot detail)

First Tree, the prime growth from which all the village originated, fell victim to a strange rot that could not be cured.

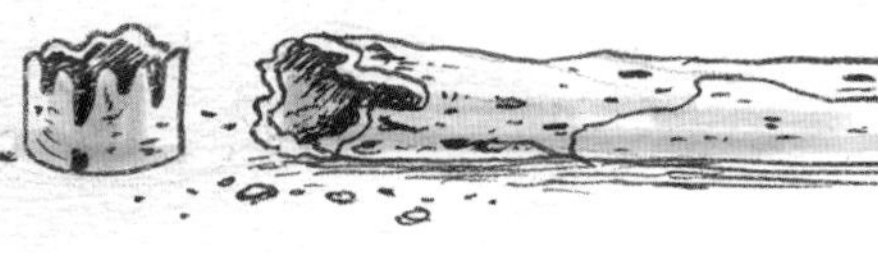

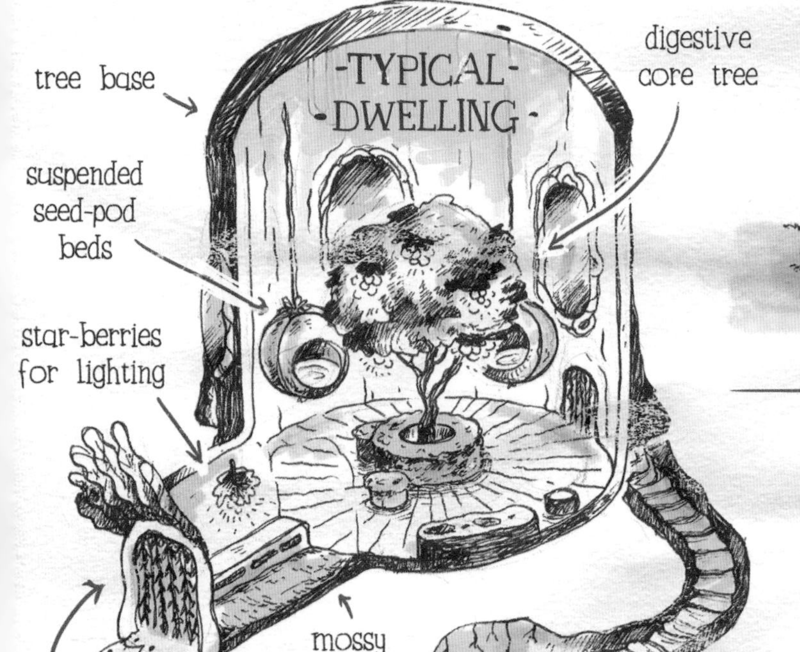

many-hands style

two-friends style

BRIDGES

pose unique challenges for negotiations as they require agreement between groups of plants that may have developed a fondness for being apart. Bridging smaller, newer gaps should prove no problem. The challenge increases with the size and age of the gap, along with the natural temperament of the plant species involved.

SONG-OF-THE-EVENING
I can light a can — dle I can light a star —
both of them are won-der — ous shin-ning where they are —

Dear Diary,

Amanda still doesn't have her sceptre, David tried to get us all to go past her island again to try and get it but we ran off to the hot pools instead. It's driving him crazy. I think he went by himself to try, but its just too high up. He thinks once we get it back we can defeat the Lizards and go home.

Nathan was being such a perv clown at the pools, he can be so gross sometimes. I got told that he's going to ask me out in the future. Yuck!

That same "person", also gave me the recipe for a secret tea ingredient. I cant say who though, that's my biggest secret!

the last time we went to the island

the tree is actually waaaag taller + DEAD!

Ben David Amanda Nathan

OH YEAH!

Another awesome day, coming my way.

A little drink for you.

And for me...

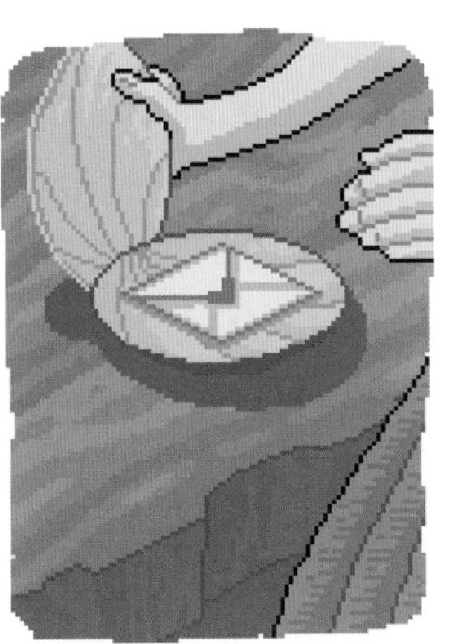

The most unforgettable day of my life.

Ha Ha Ha.

♫ Peach all day and then Peach all night. ♫

♫ Cool-cool beat and I'm feeling alright. ♩

Morning, guys, any Ruby Pockets this morning?
There are a fewtle.
GREAT! You wanna stay for tea? I'm gonna brew a pot of Morning Rise.
-OOOHHH- Yes please!

Thank you, Dear Spirit, but not this morning.
What?
We are FAR too busy with deliveries and other such duties and things.

Well, ok.
Tomorrow then, guys?
Book me in!
Bye.

NOM
-NOM-
NOM
s'good.

Hmmm...

Looks interesting.

WHAT?
NOTHING!
I wasn't doing anything.
I didn't say you were doing anything.
I said it 'looks interesting.'
Have they changed the recipe of the Starry Buns?

Ha Ha Ha WHAT?
Yeah... do you, uh, want a cup of tea?
I made a pot of Morning Rise.
Your brew? No thanks.

Gotta get in some practice for the Festival, eh?
No.
My tea-chnique is perfect, Nathan.
Per-fect.

Alright, here goes...

Hey Lilly, I've been thinking -
Like, maybe we're supposed to be here.

I know David and Amanda are trying their hardest to get back...
...but I think this is our destiny.

The PEACHES are right. Why else would we be here otherwise?
We ARE forest spirits. Not exactly the ones they want, but close enough.

I feel like this place is right and that I can be me and that's ok.
And you being here as well is right, and we're right together.
I was hoping, maybe we can take a few Thunder Birds and a picnic out beyond the wall today.
SURE!

WHAT?
Yeah sure, let's go!
David?
I'm sick of waiting around...
ERRR...

Those Peaches are keeping SECRETS from us!
I heard Ben has been sneaking out behind the wall!
Let's find out what they're hiding!

. . .

Where'd Lilly go?
Didn't she say something about having to be at the hatchery this morning?

Let's pack our bags, grab the best food and get outta here!

What about the others?
Shouldn't we get them?

NO WAY!
Like you said, just us two!
Lilly has already gone for the day.
Ben's gone out before anyway, and Amanda would NEVER come.
She doesn't even like leaving the TREE-HOUSE!
That's not fair, Amanda is just –

COMPLETELY USELESS!
Why's it up to ME to get her sceptre down from that stupid tree?
Nobody else seems to even be trying to get home!
I'm FED UP, man. It's time to BUST OUT and get some answers!

I'll go get my stuff.
Meet you back down here in five.

We'll leave the fire rocks behind for maximum sneak.

AWWW CRAP...

So, what's your plan for getting past the weaving?

Don't Thunder Birds guard the wall? Storming up and down the track.

Lilly says they RIP apart ANY animal that gets caught in the weaving.
Just like, tear their GUTS right out.

Have you SEEN the claws on them?
VICIOUS
SAVAGE
NASTY!

WONDEROUS!
Oh yeah, 'WONDEROUS'.

I don't get why we're not allowed through. They think we're the Spirits of the Forest, but won't let us into the actual forest?

We should go through here.
Check the fields by the river. Maybe even that Stone Forest we saw on the map.

Look at all this. How did BEN even get through here?
I asked him to take me with him next time he goes.
He said he didn't know what I was talking about.

HOWEVER, I've got a plan, something I've been practicing.

WELL I'VE GOT A SWORD!
NO! You idiot.

The bells will go off if you so much as touch the weaving.
UH..
Then the bird'll come and eat. YOU. ALIVE.

You sure? CHOPPY! CHOPPY!
Just watch.

Alright then, little plant...

Yes?

WELL?

My sword would have been quicker.

I've been whispering to the weaving almost since we got here.
It wouldn't even listen to me at first.

It was grown to protect the village. It takes its job PRETTY seriously.
You're TALKING to it?

But now, I think we're friends. It trusts me.
I think we can come out here whenever we want.
It sure is MESSY out here.

There are no Fire-Rocks out here to clean up the leaf-litter.
-BLAH-
It's like, as soon as the weaving stops, the Peaches stop caring!

That's way harsh, David.
PFFT
People only say that when it's way true.

How's your tea going for the Festival?
I can't believe your STUPID tree-talking stuff actually works!
We can come out here whenever we want, looking for Laurence.

Laurence?
I keep asking around the village but no one can give me a clear answer on where he is.

HEY! what's that?
HUH?

WOW...

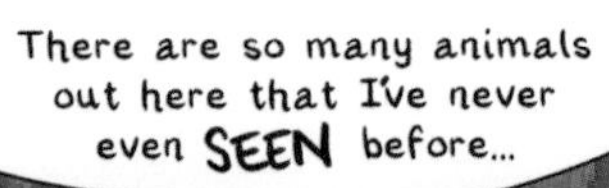
There are so many animals out here that I've never even SEEN before...

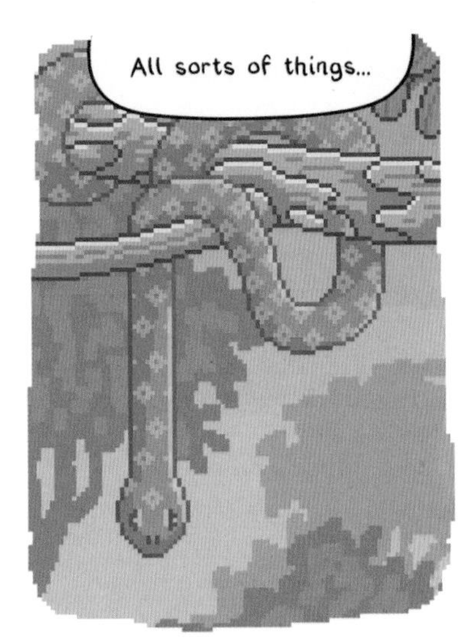
All sorts of things...

The wall must do a pretty good job of keeping them out.

Those ones look like tiny kangaroos or —

SOMETHING!

WAGH H!
ARGH!

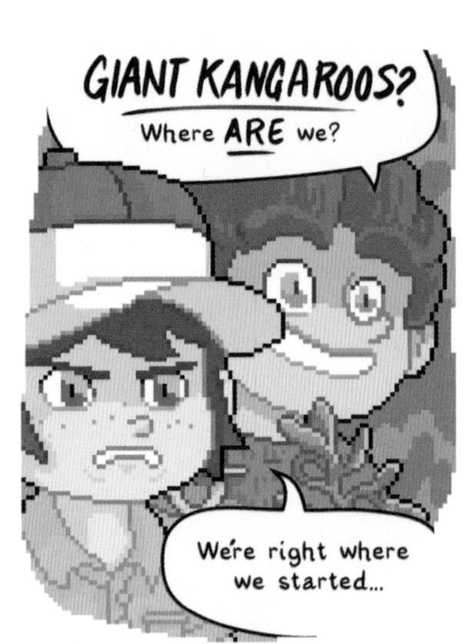
GIANT KANGAROOS?
Where ARE we?
We're right where we started...

Since we got here... I mean...when we first got here, I noticed the stars.
On the first night.
WHAT?
YEAH...
The stars here are all exactly flipped versions of the ones back home!

SOOOOO...
`SO'?
So it means PROBLEM: we can't just walk ourselves home.
And THAT means people can't just walk to US!

We're not just on the same planet we were before, but we're at the exact same coordinates...
You can't figure all that out!
I CAN and I DID!

NAH,
that doesn't make any sense, David.
You gotta relax, man!

You're just trying to make it fit into your dorky science world.
Take a look around you...
It's not like that.
OH WHAT?
So you can talk to trees but I can't track the stars?!

Well you're WRONG! You can't possibly be seeing all that!

WELL I'M RIGHT!
And that's not ALL I can see.
Your banana slug is hanging out of your pants!

WHAT?

ARGH!
YEAH...
Sorry `bout that.

Why are you even wearing those Peach clothes?
Where are your real clothes?

What do you mean?
Lilly and Ben wear Peach clothes all the time.
It's just YOU and Amanda and even-
IT'S NOT RIGHT!

SHHHHHHH
Did you hear that?
Don't try to change the subject!
SHHHH!

OOOOF!
GET IN!

Well, he's not going to put up with their Chitty-Chitty ways anymore-
Are you Serious? Maleleuca is going to be SO Fire-Stone when -

When WHAT? When he finds out? We'll be HEROES when he finds out.
`HEROES'? DEAD heroes, if it all goes to rot.

You two poor delicate petals. Ya just need some more salt in ya.
Come listen to what they have to say. You'll see!

They're not allowed out past the weaving!
It looks like they have 0% care for that rule...

What are they doing out here?

Nathan... what the FLIP is that?

It's a PYRAMID, David.
IDIOT!

I know it's a PYRAMID!
But who built it?
The Peaches sure don't have glass or metal or...

This is AWESOME!
You're not listening...

SHHHH-
I'm trying to listen.

APRIL
XVIIII

It's not enough that we go it alone-
-although some of you might be thinking that is the best of plans.

It's crotchety RIVER ELDER!
What in the Hundred Acres?

We need to send these FALSE SPIRITS back to the bottom of the river where they came from!

I have never seen them perform a single miracle.
OR tell me a single thing I didn't already know myself.

Some of you might be looking with milk-stained eyes.
FOOLS!
Their minds still half-on the vine.
But ME and YOU, we see the REAL in the matter!
The Weaving might save us from the Lizards, but we already have an enemy within our homes.

And Maleleuca would have us sway, like grass in the wind, to suit EVERYONE'S needs but our OWN!

The WEAVING isn't for us. We River Peaches sail beyond it EVERY DAY. Those rules and laws aren't for us!
Maleleuca is a weak fool who would have us live like SAPLINGS!

It's time for us to RECLAIM this forest, this ENTIRE forest!
We will turn out all the Spirits and Lizards and Tall-Fellas and grow WILD and PROUD!

They're planning on -
SHHHHHH!

They're planning on sending us HOME!
They're planning on KILLING us.

Send us back. He said they wanted to help.
Are you KIDDING ME?
Did you hear a word of-

We need to go and talk to them!
NONONONONO

STOP! Are you CRAZY?

STAY STILL!
OW!
STOP SHOUTING!
LET GO OF

THEY'RE GONNA HEAR YOU!
GET OFFA ME!
Can someone go see what that is PLEASE!

HEY!
WHO'S THERE?
We gotta get outta here NOW!

COME OUT COME OUT.

FLY, YOU FOOL!

Don't be SHY!
We just want to PLAY!

Ha Ha
Slow down, wontcha?

HA HA HA HA HA!

Come back!
FASTER!

Keep a PEEP open.
Dont lose it!

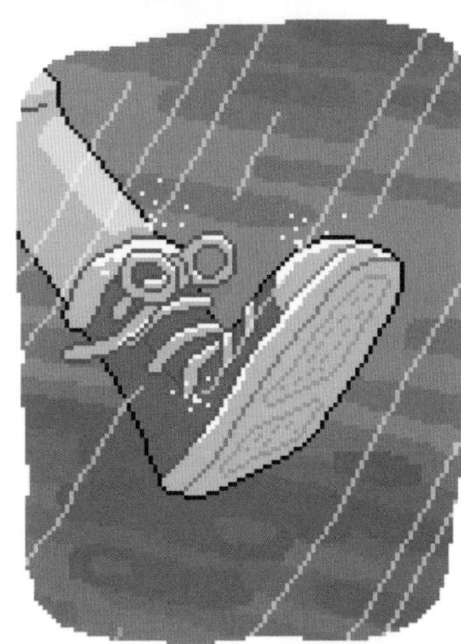

We got you NOW!
Ha Ha Ha

WA-HOOO!
Quick-sticks!

Now it's FUN TIME!
RUN
RU

OHHHH DEAR...
Youre in the WETLANDS now...
Nowhere left to RUN to...
Nowhere left to HIDE...
OHHH NO...
Maybe theyre not really trying to help us out...

♫ We're gonna catch you ♫

- and peel you like an EGG.

Ha Ha Ha
We got LOTS of time.

I can cut them down. I can do it I can -
SHHHHHH..
Why not? Cmon.

It'll be quick!
The sword is so sharp it'll-
HUSHH...

SHHHHHH.

Just a quick little game.

YOU lost it! Elder will be criss-cross with you.
Lost it.

NO WAY!
It's gotta be here somewhere.
You really lost it.

What about in here?
I did not.
I wasn't even seeing it anyway.
I was just following YOU TWO!

Nothing.
REALLY?
I wasnt seeing anything either.
There was something.
Elder saw it.
I don't know what though

We better get back. It's not safe this close to the STONE FOREST.
Probably just a roo, caught in the ivy.

Ha Ha Ha.
You wuss.
Gives me the creeps.

I THINK...
I'm pretty sure they were trying to KILL US!

BUT...
The Peaches don't kill anything...
It's all tea, meditation and craft fairs.
That was CRAZY!

This is SECRET-PLOT CENTRAL!
Remember in that episode of FABRIC ROBOTS where Tech-Swan was betrayed by the engineers even though the whole time you thought they were on the same team? The engineers had been building him every episode but really they were replacing his gears with PLASTIC ONES so that he would fall apart during his big battle with the Towering Bell. And then the big battle happened and they FINALLY revealed they were actually SPIES for the Towering Bell squadron the WHOLE TIME!

It's JUST LIKE THAT!
Yes, Nathan, it's exactly like that...
or at least SOMETHING like that.

We need to tell Maleleuca.
TELL HIM WHAT?
OH, by the way, Mal, we snuck out past the Weaving and saw some CRAZY Peaches plotting to KILL us and all the Lizards and–

–then we ran into the Stone Forest...
The what?

–and we saw all the olden days buildings.
Huh?

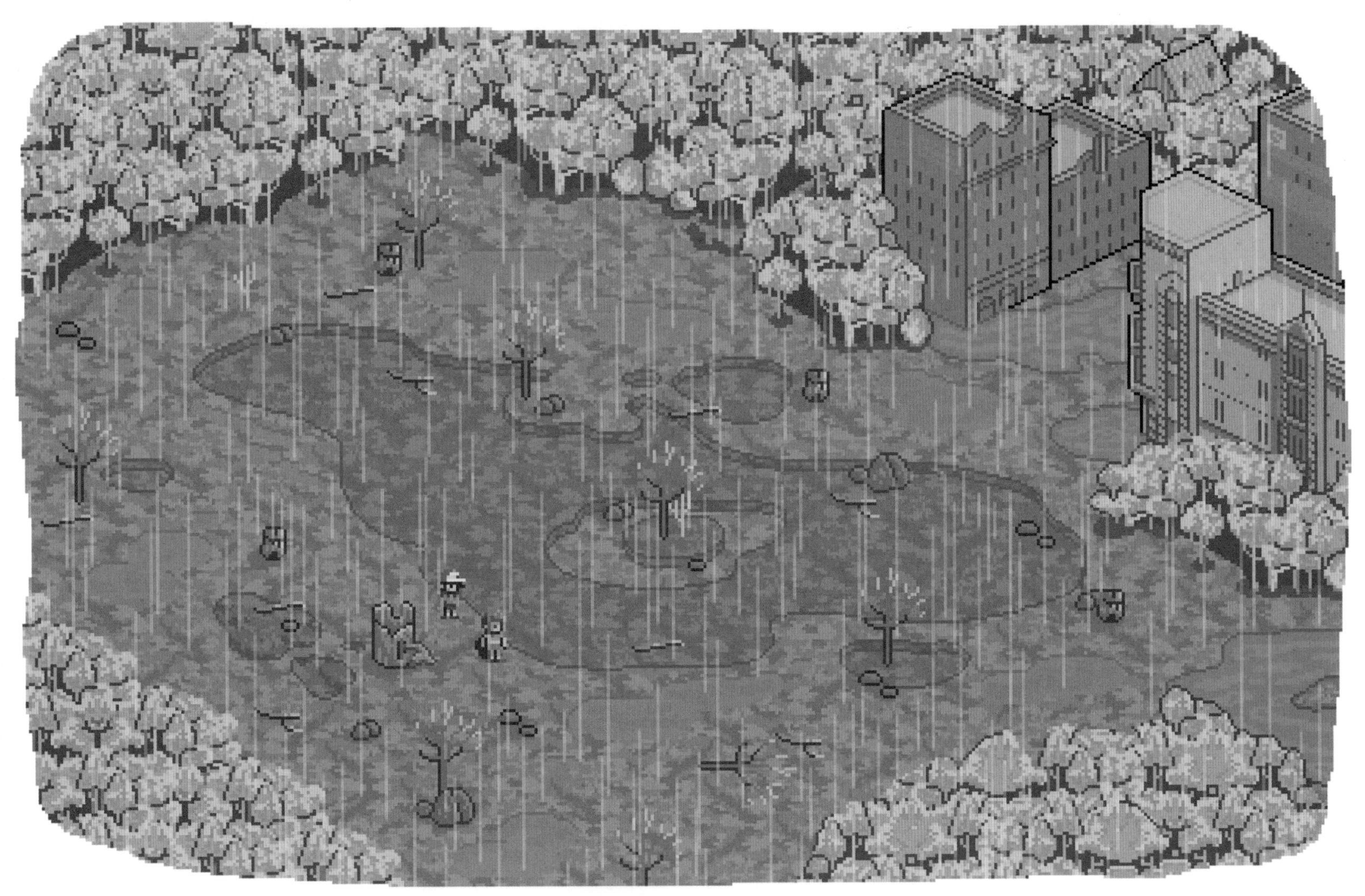

This is AWESOME!
This is INSANE!

Why didn't they tell us this was all here?
There might be clues to help us get home!

These same constellations, the old buildings... is the river the same? All those old socks and bottle-tops...?

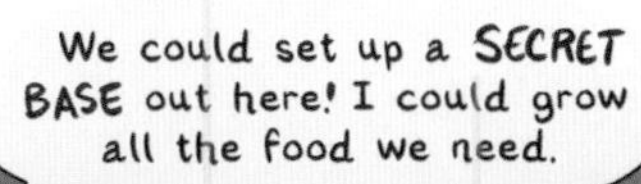

We could set up a SECRET BASE out here! I could grow all the food we need.

E R
PERTH

GC&H.SNOWBALL&Co
AHERN'S – AHE

Fish and chips.
Freezies.
Golden Gay Times!
Um, Summer Rolls.
Hamburgers!
I dunno, the Violet thing?
Violet Crumble!
Yeah, I think so... I can't remember...
Hawaiian pizza!
I'm out.
WHAT? That's it?

I just, there's just not... I don't feel like anything.
I can't really remember much from back there.
Are you SERIOUS?

I remember things, I just don't remember EVERYTHING. Not ALL of it.
You know when you have a weird dream and you're trying to remember it after you've woken up and you're trying so hard...

But before you know it, you're eating breakfast and getting ready and with each second you're forgetting more and more.

And you think, OH, if I could just get a grip on it, I could pull the whole dream back.
But then, it stops being so important, and by lunchtime...
...you've forgotten you ever had a dream at all.

I can't NOT remember.
But I'm here with all my favourite people and my BEST FRIEND and-

Who's your best friend?

OH yeah!
You too, I was just messing with your head-brain.
HaHaHa...

I don't think Laurence fell in the river with us.

No way, the Peaches SAID they saw him.
Maleleuca SAID he might be out here for all we know.

No, David, I remember seeing him on the bridge.

He didn't fall in.

WHO KNOWS what those Peaches actually know.
We could TOTALLY live here.
Look at ALL this CRAZY they've kept under lock and key.

We're NOT living here. We're NOT living with the Peaches either.
We're waiting.
Waiting until they send us back or we find a way to escape.
'Escape'?

HOLD ON.
You don't want to go home...
do you?

I just don't think we need to be MISERABLE while we ARE here.
You REALLY think we ARE Spirits!?
ARE YOU KIDDING!?

This has been an AWESOME day of adventure. That's how I'd like it remembered.
Officially.
On the record.

My mind has NO IDEA what those words even mean.
OFFICIALLY.

NO IDEA!
OFFICIALLY!

I guess we'd better get back.
Before it gets dark.

I can't believe we didn't find a single person here.
We need to talk to MAL about all this bull-crap!

Tell Mal?
David, uh, WAIT! What, what if he's in on it? RIGHT?

In on WHAT? The River-Elder said he was
DAVID!

Who knows who we can trust.
RIGHT?
I mean, maybe they're hiding ALL KINDS of things from us! Maybe they're ALL in it together!

Until we can be sure, we'd better just keep all this to ourselves.

In fact, we better just keep it between you and me. We can't even be sure we can trust the others to keep quiet!
The 'others'?

The other Spirits.

I guess you're right...

You and me, we gotta stick together, David.

Remember, not a word to ANYONE.

Geez, I'm glad I can at least trust you, Nathan.

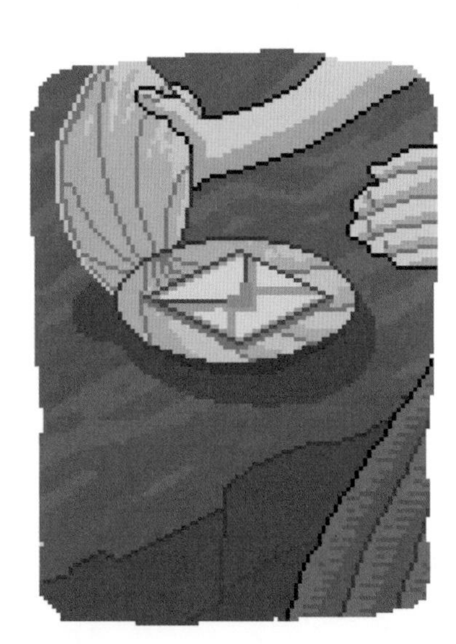

Dear Diary,
Happy Crackling Sunday! When all the baby Thunder Birds hatch for the year. It was pretty gross when they first came out but once they're dry they're *Sooooo CUTE*.
I tried to get Amanda to come but she barely leaves her seed pod let alone our tree house any more.
I spent most of the afternoon thinking about Mum and Dad. Amanda and David are always talking about home, I miss it and everything but... I dont think about it as much as them.
Dad
Mum
I guess seeing all the baby birds and their parents made me think of the

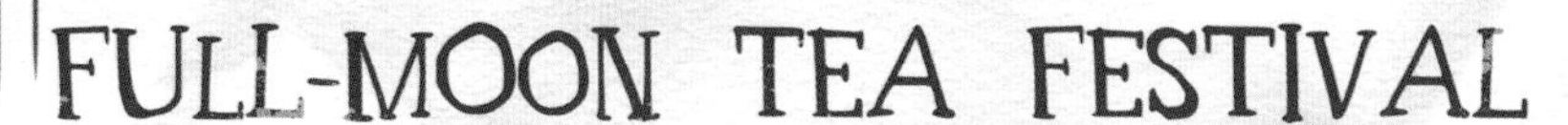

FULL-MOON TEA FESTIVAL

On the full moon of the fifth month, the Peaches hold their largest celebration of the year. While festivals and ceremonies are held on nearly a weekly basis, the FULL-MOON FESTIVAL is of greatest importance as it is in honour of the pouring of tea. Each Guild is responsible for presenting a new tea, which is judged by all the Guild Elders. Traditionally, creatures from outside the village are included, such as the Lizards.

CELESTIAL SIGNS

It is believed that the waxing and waning of the moon represents the filling and emptying of a tea cup.

THE GREAT POURING

Peaches claim to be able to see the shape of a pouring teapot in the patterns on the moon. I find that a little challenging.

TEA * POTS

Come in all shapes, sizes and adornments. While the GUILD OF MUD craft a great many tea pots, most Peaches prefer to sculpt their own pots. It is a source of pride and yet another opportunity for them to express their creativity and personalities.

Different cups and pot styles are often associated with specific teas. This is very complicated and difficult to keep track of.

* BING - BANG - BO *

When young Peaches begin to ripen, they start preparations for leaving home. This is known as the great Bing-Bang-Bo, which occurs at the beginning of the new year. These Peaches are expected to make their first tea set as a ritual. It is often looked back on with great humour and affection in later life.

BREWING

Teas are brewed over a FIRE-ROCK in special cradles. Brew time, flame intensity and brew pots vary greatly between different tea blends.

FIRE-ROCKS are very skilled at maintaining a consistant temperature and knowing when a tea is ready.

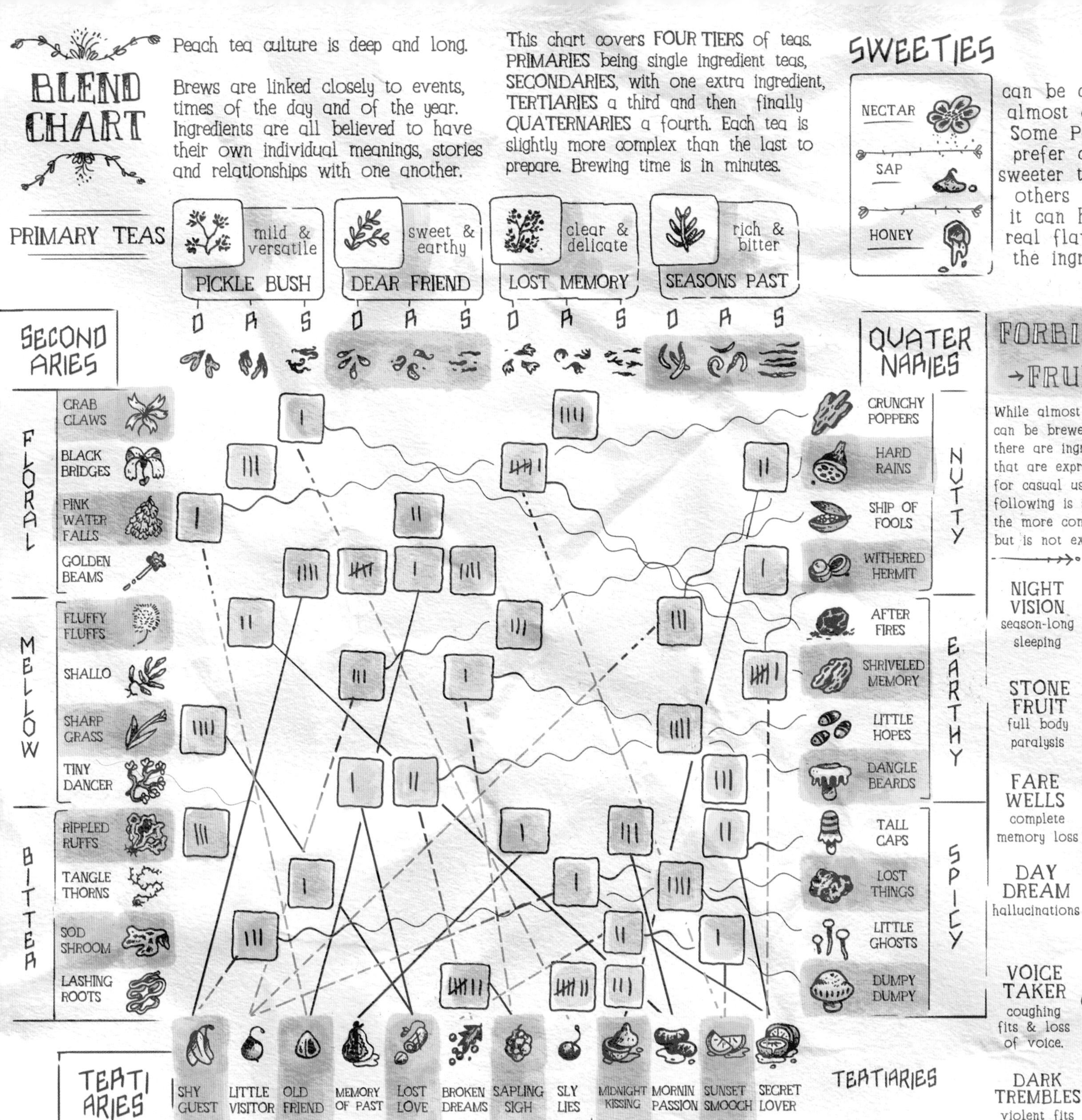

FORBIDDEN FRUITS

While almost anything can be brewed into tea, there are ingredients that are expressly banned for casual use. The list following is some of the more common ones but is not exhaustive.

NIGHT VISION
season-long sleeping

STONE FRUIT
full body paralysis

FARE WELLS
complete memory loss

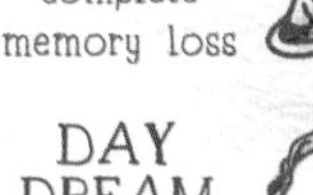

DAY DREAM
hallucinations

VOICE TAKER
coughing fits & loss of voice.

DARK TREMBLES
violent fits and sweats

the grumpiest peach in all the village
thunder bird racing (lilly won)
sky kite festival
me and Blaze
chillin like a villain
Amandas birthday (I made the cake)
spirit fans dressed up as us!
Alright ghost fans!

SONG-OF-THE-MORNING
Bless-sings on the blo — ssoms
bless-sings on the fruits ——
bless-sings on the leaves & stems &
bless-sings on the roots ——

Yes, yes.

Good morning,
you two.

Fruit market.

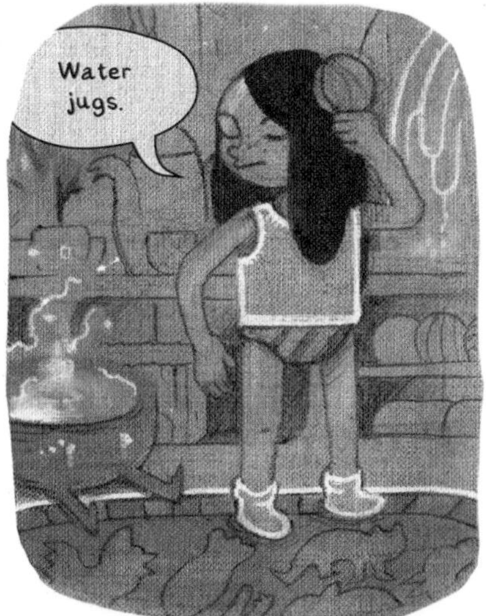
Water jugs.

New plans.

Drowned tea.

Don't even start nagging me until I'm dressed, Pepu.

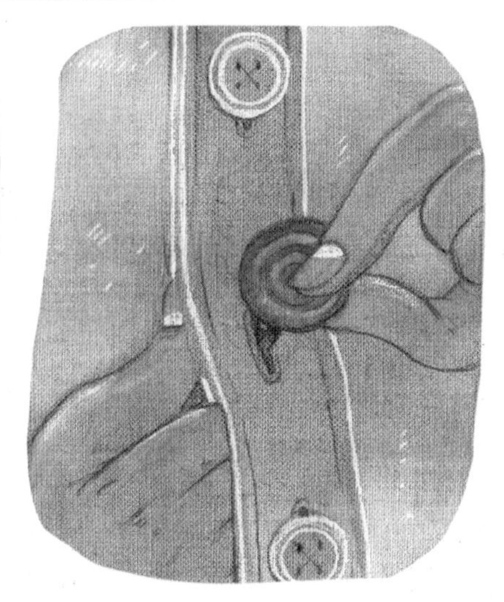

NO nonsense today.
I've got a lot to concentrate on already.

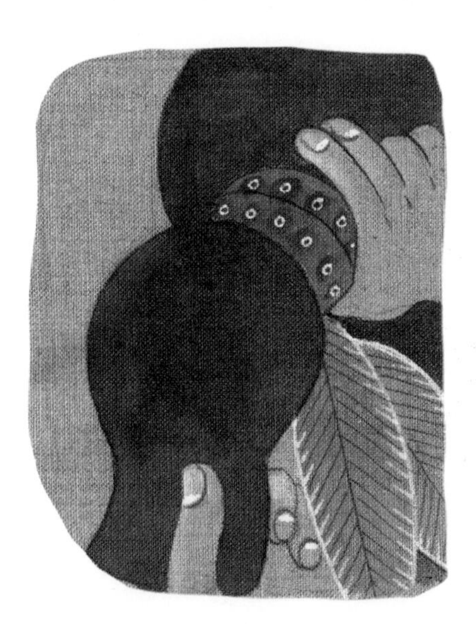

I'm not in the mood for any of your antics.

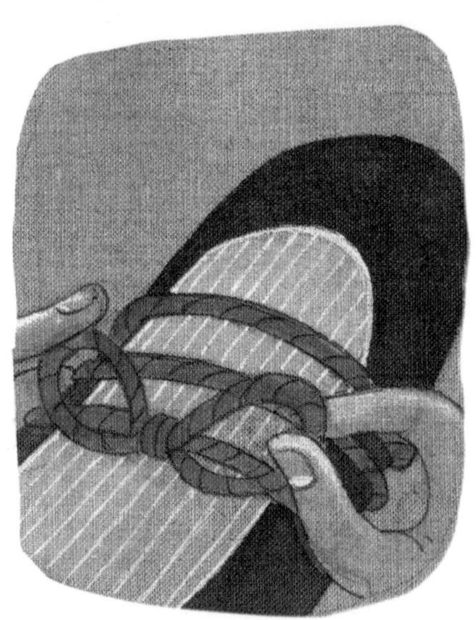

Amanda BETTER NOT be sleeping in...
Probably got her BUTT in the air, snoring away...
I TOLD her we had to be up early.
Is she on her way?

She'll be down in a few seconds, you say?
That's the FIRST straight answer I've gotten out of you ALL MONTH!

And now, what about today?
Are you going to tell me exactly how it's all going to happen?

How WHAT'S going to happen?

The Festival?
Did I hear you talking about-
YAAAW...
NOTHING, sleepy-head.
Are you ready?

READY?
NO.
WHY did you want me up SOooo early?

GOOD.
LET'S GO!

BREAKFAST!

I packed it already.
AWWW...

You can be so much like your stupid brother sometimes.

Have you noticed how cold it's getting in the mornings?

Have you?

Have I what?

Nothing...

Did you hear that BEN has been SNEAKING out past the Woven Wall?
We're TOTALLY not allowed to do that!

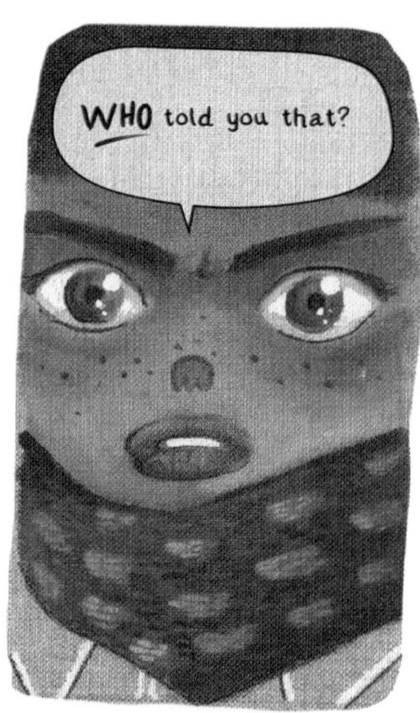
WHO told you that?

My Elder, they heard it from one of the Bakers who was—
YOUR Elder should stop gossiping!

Why didn't you tell me?
I only found out yesterday.
I didn't have a chance...

...never tell me anything useful...

What's he doing out there?
Is he getting secret ingredients for his tea as well?

Have you seen David's BOOK that he's been working on? It's really-
Excuse me, are you Bessie?
Yes.
Great, can you organise fifty buckets of water to be arranged around the main stage for tonight?
Forty?

Do you know that Peach?
No.
Anything you say, Dear Spirit.

Oh, and have you seen what Nathan has been growing in the -

AMANDA, STOP.

JUST. STOP.
No boys.
Remember?

SOZ.
We've got a lot of work to do for the Festival.

I just want to have a great day with you.
Ok?

Are you ok, Lil?
I mean, apart from being stuck in this forest...

Lil?

Just one good day, while we still can.

THE TENTH

What can I give you for the Sunset Fruit Cuts?
Give me? I couldn't possibly-

Please.
Let me at least give you this.

A FOOT POUCH?
Dear Spirit, you're much too kind!

Thanks, Dew Dew.
See you at the tea festival tonight?
Hey...
Betcha blossom you will!

What's Nathan growing over there? A maybepole or something...

Yes yes.
It's a MAYpole. He's very clever. But no boys.
Sorry.... I forgot.

So, how's your tea recipe coming along?
Uh...

I, uh, well...
I haven't exactly, really started.

AMANDA!
The Peaches are expecting you to have a tertiary tea.
You've had weeks!
'scuse me.

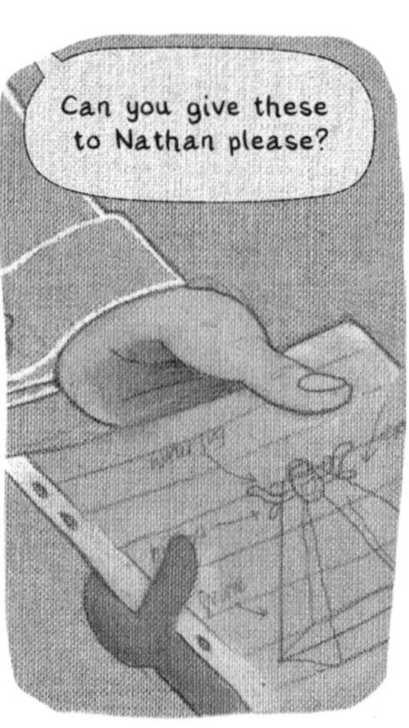
Can you give these to Nathan please?

They're the new plans for the maypole.

Sure thing.

UH, Lil,
let's go a different way...

Hello there.

Are YOU wanting to step your rancid milk-stained feet on MY BEACH?

Can we go another way? pleeease?

I don't know WHO you're used to talking to like THAT,
but it's NOT ME.

Stand in my way again and I'll have the river crabs EAT YOU ALIVE while you're sleeping.

You don't have that power.
You're not a REAL SPIRIT!

Aren't I?

Hold this, would you?
Ok.
If he comes back, just throw rocks at him.
Lil, what are you DOING? It's so cold.

LILLY?

LILLY!

Got it.

That water is FREEZING, Lilly.
Put your cloak back on!

Have a look.
It's for my tea.

Juice-plums steeped in salted river-water for one moon cycle.

It STINKS!
No one's gonna drink that.
I found the secret recipe one day while helping in the hatchery.
A mother-bird had used the recipe scroll to pad out her nest.

Y'know, it was here that they pulled us out.

Right here.

WHAT?
NONE of us remember that. Even YOU said so!

I remember the water, after the bridge broke.

Filling my lungs. So cold.
Sometimes...
Sometimes it, the blackness, the cold...

I didn't know...

How are we gonna get your sceptre?

I dunno.
Do you even care?

OF COURSE!

It sort of doesn't seem like you really care.

I just want to go home.
I'm so tired.
I just want David to -

David's not going to get us home.

He's not your boyfriend, either.

GEEZ, WEIRD!
Why would you even SAY such a RANDOM thing?
HA HA HA HA

Heh heh heh...

You can see it from here...

When the sun hits it right.

I've stood here and wondered about it.
WHY is your sceptre all the way up THERE?

I mean, they told us it fell from the sky during a big storm...

But really, why?
Sometimes it feels like all this, EVERYTHING is nothing but make-believe.

Do you want to go home?

It's been six months now.

Well, do you?

I don't want to play this STUPID game anymore!
I just want to go home and watch TV, Lil.

I'm TIRED of pretending.
I'm tired of how DIRTY everything is and how cold it is and how hot it is and how all the days are SOOOOO booooring...

Relaxing.

And we're all so scared...

Not everone is scared, Amanda.

I mean...

I KNOW what you mean.

It's just,
you're ALL so into it. You all act like you LOVE this place.
Catching fish and roasting things and weaving stuff and...

I don't know how much longer I can do this for...

Give me a hand.
We've been gone for SO LONG. My mum...
She probably thinks I'm DEAD!

Your mum will be freaking out.

Remember your tenth birthday at Sizzler, when we made that THREE-TIER dessert?

And when we were walking back to the table, we TRIPPED 'cos we were laughing so hard and it FELL in that BABY-STROLLER!

Your MUM was squealing and called off the whole sleep-over and sent us all home.

Ha Ha Ha Ha Ha.
Yeah, good times.

I guess...
It's just so...
It's all like a BAD DREAM.

It's not a dream, Amanda.
You can't share a dream.

I remember this dream-
HA HA HA
No, wait, it wasnt a DREAM, it was a TV show.

And there was an ocean, an ocean UNDER the ocean.

Right under there. It had TIDES and WAVES and FISH in there and EVERYTHING!

It was AMAZING!

A lake under the ocean?
YEAH!

Do you want some?
Fruit cuts. My favourite.

HEY!
Save some for me!
Oh HI, Mal.

OM-NOM
NOM-NOM
sgood.

SAY, arent you supposed to be getting ready for the festival?

Oh, but I most certainly am.
Look at ME, standing here in preparation.
So VERY preparing.

Right here, I am checking the progress of your teas.

AH, the unmistakable smell of moon-rot.

Could that be woven sea grass-beads?

And of course, roasted pep-seeds.
How did you know?!
Is he right?

All classic ingredients. All good choices.

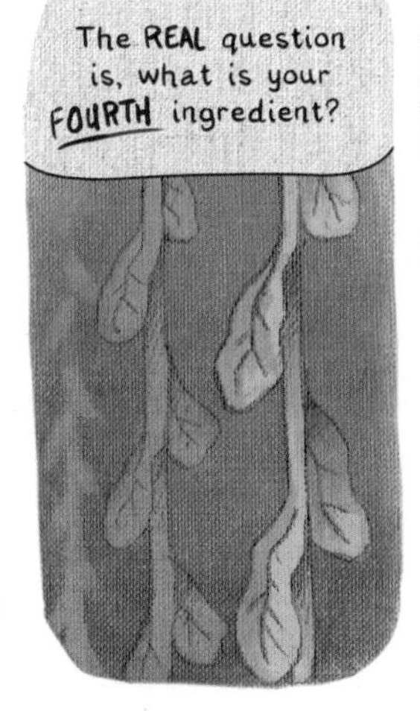
The REAL question is, what is your FOURTH ingredient?

NO CHANCE, Mal, it's a secret.

As it should be.

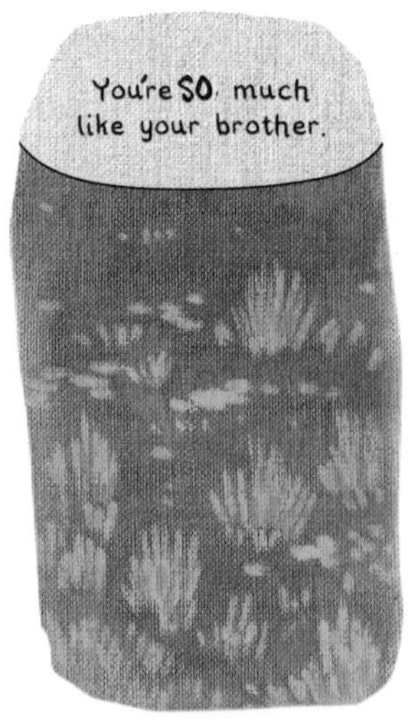
You're SO much like your brother.

You mean he's just like ME!
I was born forty minutes before him.

SO MUCH like him.

YOU IN THERE, MALELEUCA?

OOPSIE-DAISY! I've been caught. Better get back!
Bye.
Seeya.

Tea's done!

ERR, OK...
Don't worry, you little bogue. I KNEW you hadn't been working on your tea.
I've put together a simple blend for you, back at the tree-house.

You tell me these STUPID things, like to drown the juice-plums.

You tell me these STUPID things, like we'll never go home.
That we gotta keep pretending.

That Nathan will do this.
And David will do that.
And I can't do ANYTHING about any of it.

What I want to know is if everything is going to be alright in the end.

That's tricky.
You're being tricky again.

Tell me if everything is going to be alright in the middle.
As we go along.

IS AMANDA GOING TO BE ALRIGHT?

You tell me these THINGS and there's NOTHING I can do about it, IS THERE?

YOU WHITE DEVIL OF A THING!

YOU!

YOU!

You...

Is everything alright in there, Dear Spirit?

Yes, just...

I just need a minute.

At last!
Dear Spirit, you are looking the true embodiment of our forest friends.

Did you bring your tea?

Yes.

No, did you BRING your tea?

Oh, YOUR tea had better watch out for MY tea.

BRILLIANTFUL, a bit of healthy competition.

Everyone is in eagerment to see your teas.
ONWARD into the night!

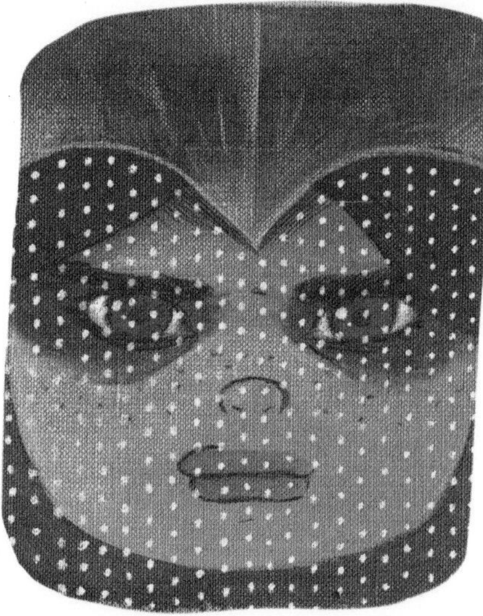

MY PEACHES RIPE! MY PEACHES SOFT!
It is, again, the most magical of nights.

It has been a MOST difficult of years.
For the first of times in many many moons, we have had to close our border to the Greater Forest.
It is with a terrific heaviness that we celebrate this Festival without our old friends, the sun catchers, the Lizard Empire.
This full moon is a time for gazing inwardly.

Where we can see in ourselves the Kindness and generosity that will allow us to REGROW!

Next year, I can see us TOGETHER again.
Drinking, laughing, trading and full of song.

SHHHHHHHH.
For we are all a part of this GREAT connection.

The Sun-Catchers, The Water-Walkers, The Stones-of-Life.
Are you ok?
He just won't shut up!

They are all us, and we in turn are all of them.
Yeah, his speeches can go on...
SHUT UP! SHUT UP!
SHUT UP! SHUT UP!

SHUT UP!

We've got to go.
What about the ceremony?

Your TEA, you've been working on it for months...

I don't care.

I just want to have this night.

One perfect night.

With you.

We're gonna be in SO MUCH trouble!

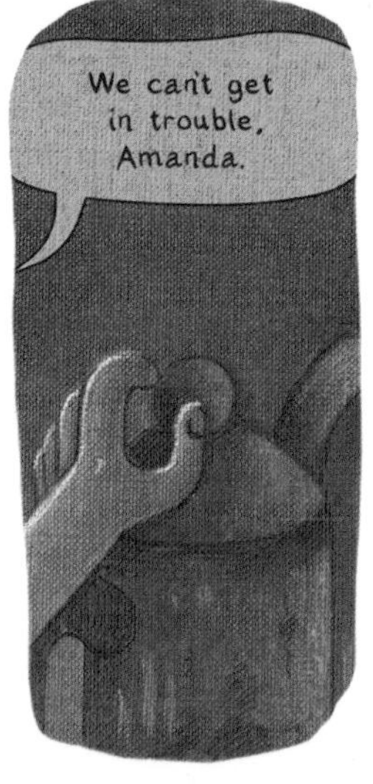
We can't get in trouble, Amanda.

We're gods.

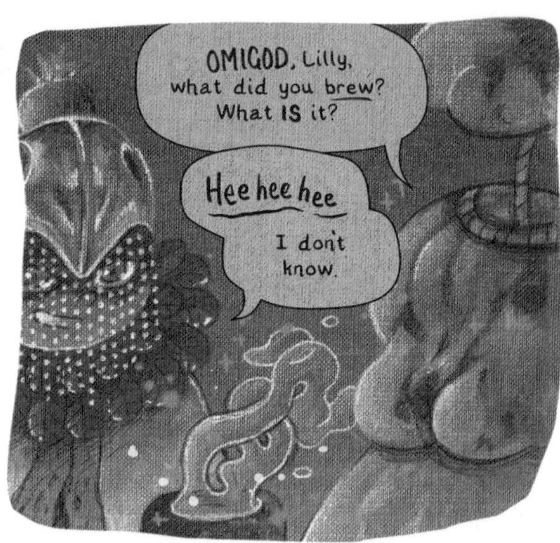
OMIGOD, Lilly, what did you brew? What IS it?
Hee hee hee
I don't know.

Hold out your cup.
You're so funny.

It's so... LOOK at all the sparkles.
It's like a HOLOGRAM!

Tastes like burnt honey.
All tingly.

Lilly?
Where are you going?

Lilly, I feel all fizzy.

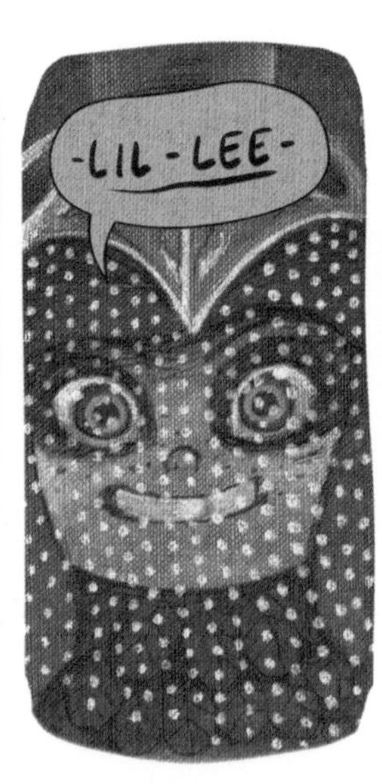
-LIL-LEE-

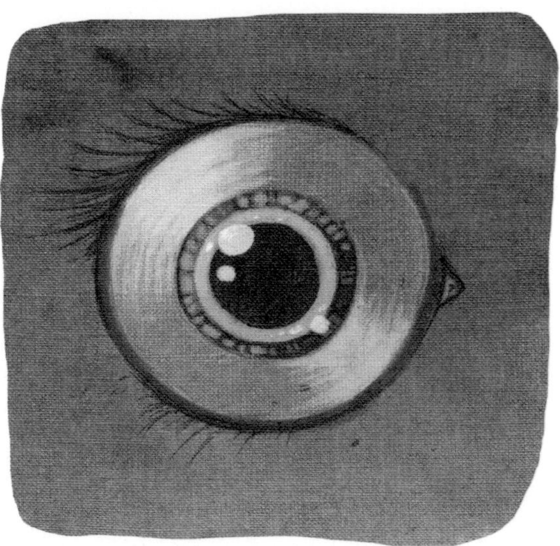

-Hee hee hee-
-HA-Hee-Hee-

Hee Hee har-kk.
Hee hee -pffff-

PRBPP
SHHHHH we can't let them hear us.

OOOPS!
SHHHHH

-YOU-

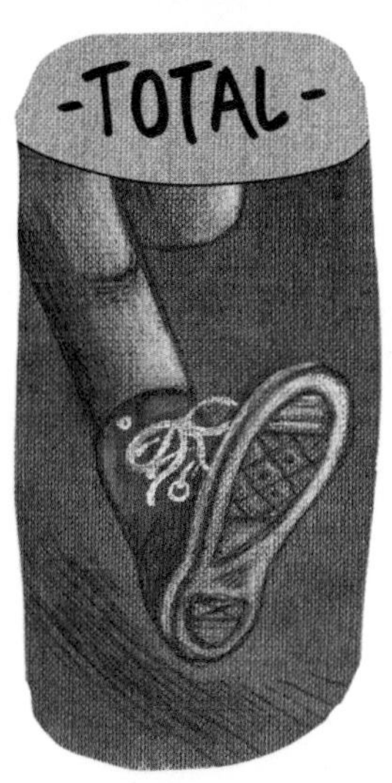
-TOTAL-

IDIOT!
Where the HELL have you been?
We thought you'd been KIDNAPPED!
Kidnapped?

The Lizards... they came to the Festival.
They set fire to everything.
All the tents and there were Peaches running around SCREAMING!

The WHOLE place went up in flames, luckily there were heaps of buckets of water just laying around that we used to fight the fire.

We chased them off, back down to the beach. They escaped through a hole in the weaving.

One of them almost got me, down there.. Had his club up and everything.
But when he went to swing it down on me, Ben fly-kicked him into the water.
Oh, Nathan.

Ben is still with him, we've got to go.
Go WHERE?
To see if he's alright!
Who?

DAVID! He's at the FIRST TREE.
He was BURNT ALIVE - haven't you been listening to me?
Oh no.

David...

You.

YOU LIED to me.

You told me AMANDA would be burnt.

I did everything to stop it, but this... this was what was going to happen all along, wasn't it?

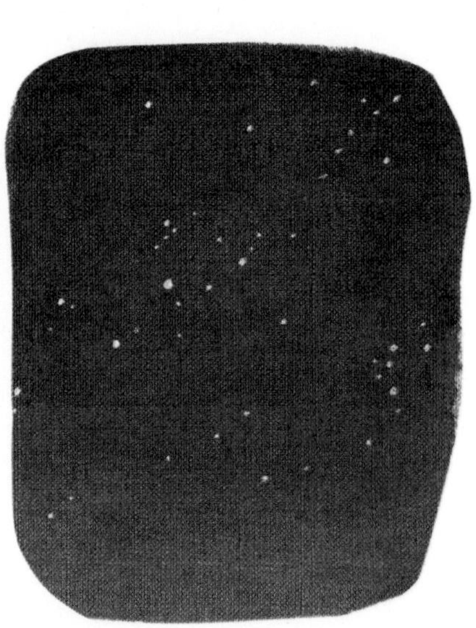

Let me through.
PLEASE...

Please, I just need to . . .

UGH.

Lilly.

Lilly, I don't think you should...
He's really badly hurt.
The mystics are saying he might not...

Ughhh-haghah..

OH, Lilly..

He's so badly burnt, Lilly...

WHAT are we gonna do?

I have a plan.

THE VILLAGE *of the* PEACHES

is perched upon the highest point along the valley.
It provides for the Peaches, and in turn the Peaches provide for it.

The soil is cared for so that it can provide enough food for all the villagers. The river is fished from, just enough, to nourish everyone. Much time is spent in celebration, dancing, performing and eating. When there is an oversupply of resources or goods, they are gifted or traded during open festivals with other groups living in the Other Lands.

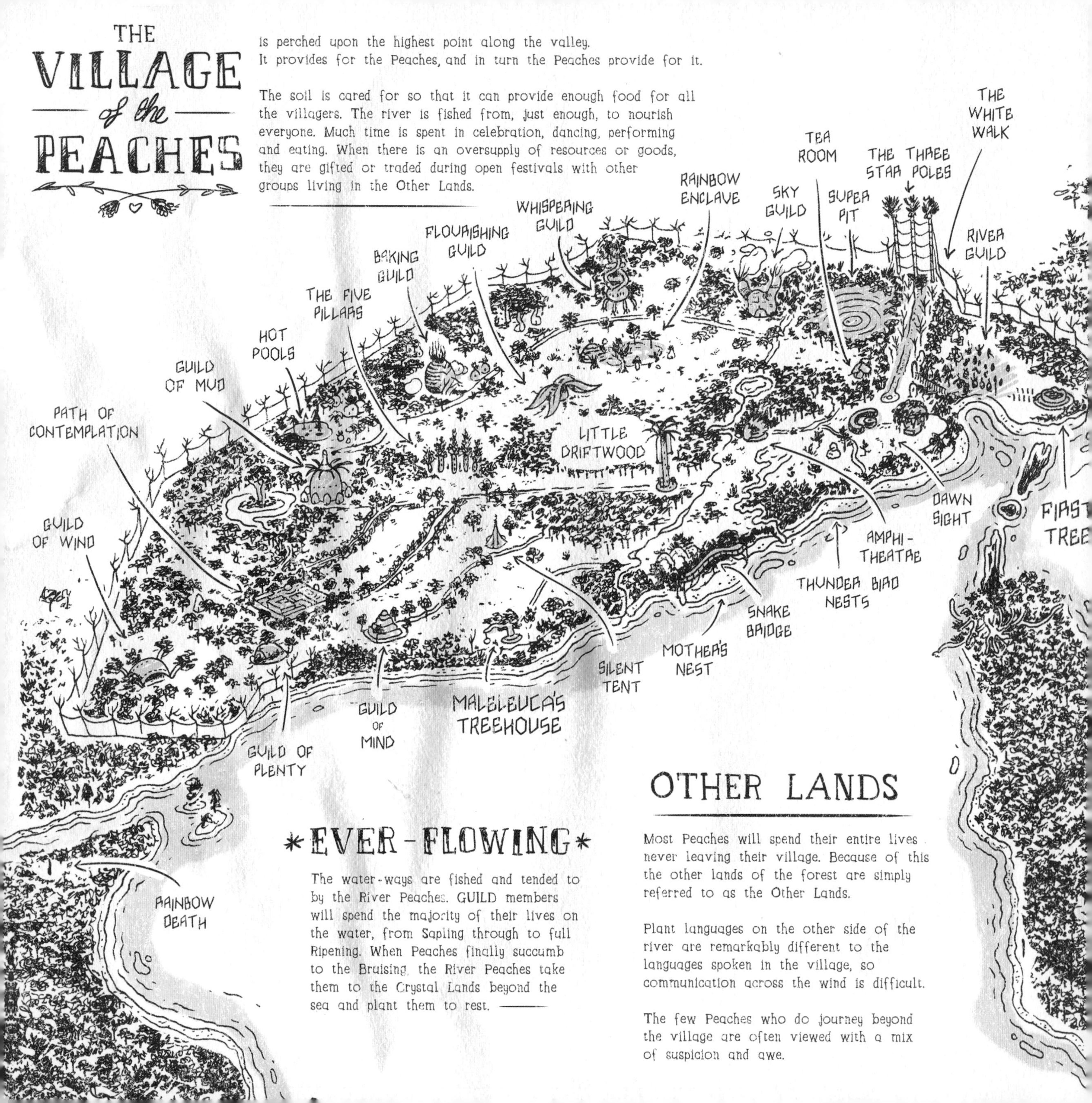

EVER-FLOWING

The water-ways are fished and tended to by the River Peaches. GUILD members will spend the majority of their lives on the water, from Sapling through to full Ripening. When Peaches finally succumb to the Bruising, the River Peaches take them to the Crystal Lands beyond the sea and plant them to rest.

OTHER LANDS

Most Peaches will spend their entire lives never leaving their village. Because of this the other lands of the forest are simply referred to as the Other Lands.

Plant languages on the other side of the river are remarkably different to the languages spoken in the village, so communication across the wind is difficult.

The few Peaches who do journey beyond the village are often viewed with a mix of suspicion and awe.

THE STONE FOREST
CRYSTAL CASTLE
WETLANDS
THE STONE FOREST
While this area is on the same side of land as the Village, the Peaches have sectioned it off and designated it as being forever forbidden. The shifting nature of its stone trees, appearing and disappearing without notice, means it is near impossible to map and incredibly dangerous to visit.
THIRD
SECOND
WHITE TREE ISLANDS
FIRST
OTHER LANDS

Nathan went fishing
Gross!
the march of seasons
check out this weird tapestry
the weaving
boat race festival
caught this butterfly hatching
a water bug snuck into the village

Dear Diary,
I have a plan.
A way to get us all home.
If I catch Pepu again I'm going to throw him in the river.
I'm going to brew some more tea and see what I can see, then tell everyone the plan
David is going to be ok.
We are all going home.
I don't know what to believe anymore.

SONG-OF-WATER

END OF BOOK ONE

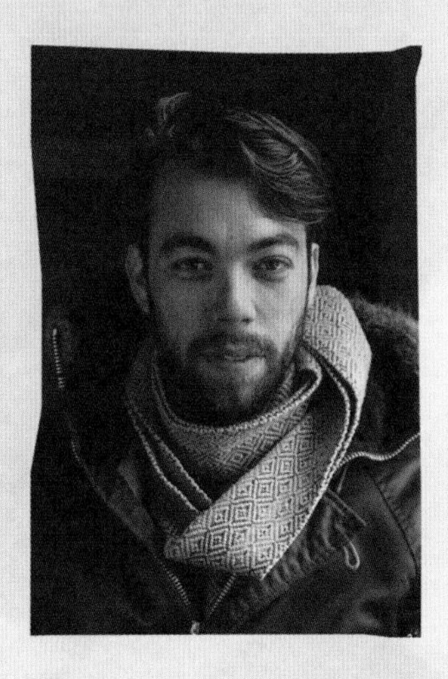

Campbell Whyte was born
in Perth, Western Australia,
wedged between a restless
ocean and an endless desert.

He began making things not
long after his birth, and today
that rich tradition continues.

Home Time combines his love
of the wild, video games,
comics and art history into
one great big adventure.

When not making comics,
Campbell runs the children's
art school Milktooth with his
wife, son and their hairless dog.

thanks to:
Mum + Dad + family for always supporting me. Tina, for unending enthusiasm. Nazario, for his patience while I worked on this book. Liz, for sharing a dream with me. Nicki, for mentoring me and encouraging this strange work. Shaun, for setting an impossibly high bar + daring me to try. Briony, for always being up for a squiggle. Chris, for taking a chance. Fred, Harry, James, for adventures. Elizabeth, for letting me into the CAW family. CAW family, for filling my heart to bursting. Alaina, for advice on paper matters. Pat, for giving me the country on the page. Luke, for registering me for the portfolio review. Ted, for taking the time to visit Perth. Leigh, for patiently combing the book. Jess, Suzanne, Robert + Luke for helping plot a course. Comics Maker Network, for boosting my morale. Apologies to everyone I forgot ...♡

Home Time would not have been possible without the generous support of the following organisations:

Photo by Gabriel Clark

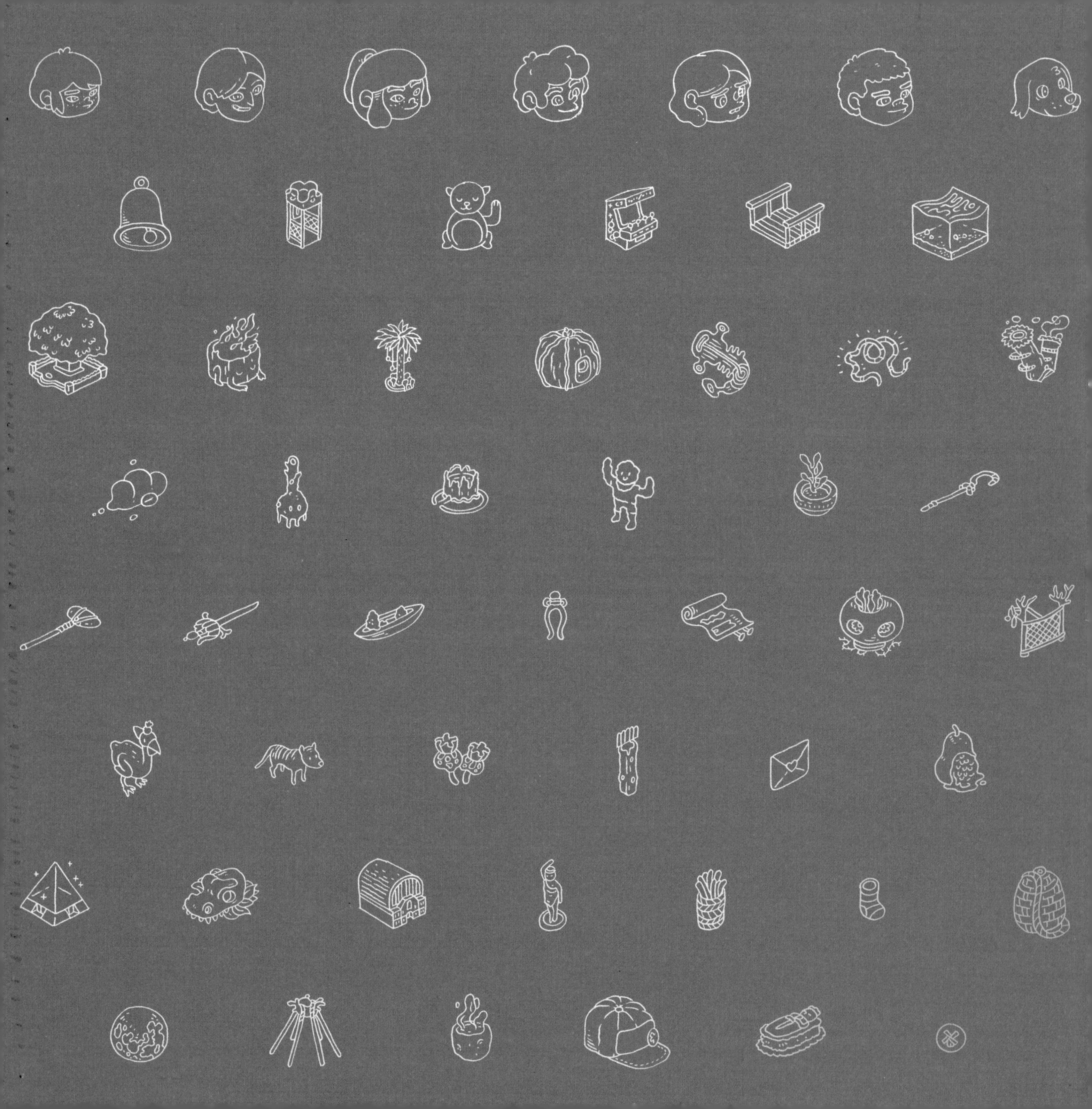